THREE RULES I'D NEVER BREAK

A SWEET ROMANTIC COMEDY

NEVER SAY NEVER
BOOK FIVE

REMI CARRINGTON

Phrey
Press

❀ Created with Vellum

How can a good guy make me want to break all my rules?

I have three rules. One I learned as a child, and the others I learned running my lingerie store. But even following my rules, I can't seem to meet the right kinds of guys. I only attract bad boys, and I'm sick of it.

When the gorgeous but incredibly shy deputy has me inadvertently breaking rule 1, I change my dating strategy. If bad boys seek me out, maybe it's time I set my sights on a good guy. And, yes, the deputy with dazzling green eyes and heart-melting smile qualifies. As for the rule-breaking, it was a one-time thing.

Eli barely speaks to me, but I'm up to the challenge.

Then I break another rule for him and start to question my assumption about good guys.

CHAPTER 1

*R*unning a business in a small town was a huge success for me. Dating in a small town… not so much. What was wrong with guys? I'd found a string of duds lately. They weren't all from the small town where I lived, but that didn't make me feel any better. In fact, it made me feel worse. Jeans and boots or suits and ties, no matter what they wore, they showed their true colors by the end of the night.

I knew better than to paint all guys with the same brush. But it seemed that most of the good ones were taken.

If good guys were out there and single, they sure weren't asking me out.

After a quick glance at my speedometer, I wiped my eyes and focused on the road.

Tonight's date was worse than the last few. Not that I went on many these days. I should've left as soon as he asked how the lingerie business was going. Shoot, I should've gotten back in my car when he'd greeted me with that icky grin. My alarms had gone off then, and I should've trusted my gut. Maybe I should add that to my rules—trusting my gut.

But I'd stayed, thinking it wouldn't be all that bad. Usually, I made it until dessert before bad dates turned south. This guy propositioned me before drinks arrived at the table. Lucky for him or he might've been wearing his.

What about me attracted the bad guys? I was a rule-follower. I didn't speed. At red lights, I stopped. When I changed lanes or turned, I used my blinker. In spite of my rule-following ways, men often made assumptions about me because I owned a lingerie store. And I hated when they did that.

With my dating track record, I chose places within walking distance, or I drove. Tonight, I'd driven, which was why I was wiping tears and trying to stay in my lane. Being so upset about it was embarrassing. It was just a bad date.

Now I was hungry, furious, and contemplating the idea of staying single. I should probably chuck my whole plan for a happily ever after. But so far, the success of my business hadn't drowned my craving for a handsome husband and, maybe someday, a family.

Nothing would choke out that desire, more accurately a need. I needed to have a career and a husband, a dog and at least one kid. Anything short of that, and I feared that I'd turn into my mother. Of all the people in the world, she was not who I wanted to emulate.

My plan wasn't going well.

Would I ever meet a man who was worth the effort of putting on heels and makeup? A guy who checked all the boxes. Someone who didn't assume that lace signaled an aversion to commitment.

Okay. Slow down. Commitment? I needed at least a first date to go well.

After exiting the highway, I drove toward Stadtburg, brushing fresh tears off my cheeks. Anger had my eyes leaking.

At the red light, I turned right, eager to be home. Just as the strip mall came into view red and blue lights flashed behind me.

Tonight couldn't get any worse.

I rolled down my window and waited, squeezing the steering wheel a little too tightly. The officer had no reason to pull me over, so now I was even more angry. That meant more tears.

Wiping my face and blinking, I smiled when he appeared at the window. Great. It was the hot one. Eli Gallagher. Most of the deputies in this county were married and/or old. This guy was neither. And my friends had been less than shy about trying to set us up. I'd be fine with that. Hello? He was extremely good-looking, and he was employed. But there was one teeny tiny problem with the setup thing.

He hardly spoke to me at social functions. He'd never pulled me over before. Maybe he was more talkative on the job.

"Evening. May I see your license and insurance please?" His brow knitted when I turned on my overhead light.

I dug through my purse, handing him what he needed as I found it. "I didn't do anything wrong."

"You failed to come to a complete stop at the red light."

"Right on red is allowed there." I blinked rapidly. "Sorry, I have something in my eye."

Tears. That was what I had in my eye. In both eyes actually.

He tapped his hand against his ticket book. "You didn't come to a complete stop before turning."

"I'm sorry you didn't think my stop qualified as complete."

He smirked. "Right." He handed back my license and insurance paper. "Miss Carter, next time please make sure you stop *completely* before turning. Tonight, I'm issuing you a verbal warning."

"What does that mean?" I thumped the steering wheel.

"It means you aren't getting a ticket, only my mini lecture on not rolling a red light."

"Thank you, Eli." That part I meant. A ticket would have made me bawl, and doing that in front of him would be horribly embarrassing.

He nodded and turned.

I started the engine, rolled up my window, and shrieked when he knocked on the glass. Trying to find the right switch, I managed to roll down all the other windows before getting the driver's side window down.

"Yes?"

He scrubbed his face, and I could see the concern swirling in his eyes. "You okay?"

All I had to do was nod and drive away, but no. I unloaded. "Are there any men in this county who don't ask out a woman, hoping for nothing more than a one-night stand? It shouldn't matter that I own a lingerie store. That doesn't mean I want… want… that!"

His eyes widened as I continued.

"Why is it that the rotten apples seek me out? All I wanted was a puppy, but I can't get one yet. And he seemed nice at first."

"The puppy?"

"The guy. We didn't even have our drinks yet when he asked me to—" I covered my face with my hands. "And now I'm making a fool of myself. I cry when I'm angry. It's like when there's a fire and the automatic sprinklers come on."

He didn't respond.

After a deep inhale and letting the breath escape, I turned to face him. "But, yeah, I'm okay."

His jaw was clenched, and anger flared in his green eyes.

What I expected to see wasn't there. Pity. There wasn't a hint of it anywhere on his face.

His head bobbed in a small nod, and he pointed at my overhead light. "It'll be easier to see if you turn off that light."

It was easier to see him with the light on. And now was when I should take a good look because after my display, he wouldn't come anywhere near me again.

I'd wager money on that.

CHAPTER 2

*S*till fuming from my bombed date, I parked in front
of the store, then marched across the parking lot
and around the building. I unlocked the back door of my
store, which also happened to be my temporary home. That
was only because my beautiful new house would be finished
in four months and my lease had ended two weeks ago. No
way was I going to sign a six-month lease just to live there
four months. The tiny apartment in the back of my lingerie
shop would do for the short term.

My phone rang as I closed the door. "What?" I didn't
normally answer the phone that way, but I'd seen who called.
Sending the call into oblivion would have been smarter, but
hearing one more apology—even a fake one—might ease a
bit of my rage.

"Don't be mad, I think we got off on the wrong foot." The
jerk sighed. "Don't be difficult. I just pulled up outside your
shop. I saw your car out front. Let's go grab a drink and talk
about it. Or I could come in…"

There were so many things wrong with what he'd said I
didn't even know where to start. It had creeped me out in the

restaurant when he'd asked about my business because I hadn't mentioned owning a lingerie store. It creeped me out even more that he'd driven to where I worked… and lived.

The name I used in my day-to-day life wasn't what was on all my official documents. My mother—God love her—was so outside the box, she wasn't aware of the box. Anyway, she chose my first name; my dad decided on my middle name. All my documents were under the name Shasta D. Carter. The D stood for Delaney. That was the name I used.

But the weirdo didn't know my name was Shasta. People who knew couldn't keep from making jokes about it.

"Not interested." I ended the call and tossed my purse on the bed. While I could act tough, my insides felt like jelly. I needed to calm down.

When I was young, I'd learned to take care of myself. That was when I learned the first rule. Then with my success in business had come challenges and creeps, and I added two more rules. Even when following all of them, I still found the bad boys. More accurately, they found me. Why? I didn't want a bad boy. But that seemed to be the only type of guy who wanted me. I guess owning a lingerie store sent that signal. Thus, the rules.

Rule one. Never get caught with your pants down. I'd learned this rule from a drunk old man outside a sketchy bar in a tiny coastal town out west. He shared the advice with me —I was only seven at the time—then promptly got in trouble breaking his own rule. Literally. Thankfully, I hadn't seen it. I'd just heard him shouting at the police about it while I hid in the back seat of my mom's car. Even as young as I was, I understood what he meant and added the second part to that rule. Always be prepared for anything.

Rule two. Never model the merchandise. This was a frequent request. Ugh. What weirdo thought I'd actually do that?

Rule three. Never date a customer. If they made their way into my shop, they were in a relationship, and I wasn't going to be an extra or a home-wrecker. And the guys who said they were shopping for their mom—liars. All of them.

I shrugged off my cute little jacket and returned it to the hanger. Piece by piece, I shed my clothes, eager for a shower to wash off the stench of the bad date. Because the only bathroom was across the hall, I wrapped a towel around me for the short trip. The windows across the front had blinds—which were closed—but I still opted for a towel because of rule number one.

I tiptoed across the dark hallway, turned on the bathroom light, and closed the door.

After turning on the shower, I pulled my hair into a ponytail, then smeared on a calming face mask. Calming probably meant it was for irritated skin, but right now, I was willing to try anything. Maybe a mini spa session in the shower would relax me. It had to.

I pulled back the curtain to step into the shower and stopped when I heard a thunk. That sounded close.

Had I forgotten to lock the door? I closed my eyes, trying to remember. The jerk had called right after I'd stepped inside. I couldn't remember if I'd locked the bolt.

I pressed my ear to the door.

Footsteps. Someone was definitely in my store.

Had that creep come in? If he'd snuck in, this wouldn't end well for him. I could call the police, but my phone was on my bed across the hall.

I needed a plan.

The bathroom didn't offer much in the way of defensive weapons. After a quick scan, I tightened the towel around me and picked up the plunger. Whoever got hit with this deserved it.

I pushed open the door and tiptoed into the hall.

"Hands up! Drop the... Delaney?" A figure stood with a flashlight in one hand and a gun in the other. The voice was all too familiar, but thankfully not the jerk's.

The plunger hit the ground as my hands shot up. Even though I knew Eli had figured out it was me, I obeyed.

The man had a gun; I had a towel.

"What are you doing here, Eli?" I glanced down as the purple Egyptian cotton towel responded ever so slightly to the pull of gravity.

Why had I thrown my hands into the air with such gusto? Keeping the rise and fall of my chest to a bare minimum, I dropped my elbows lower.

Silently, I begged the towel not to slip.

"The burglar alarm." He lowered his gun.

That was the other thing I'd forgotten. To turn off the silent alarm.

"Is there anyone else here with you?" He moved toward my bedroom door.

"There better not be. You can check." If my dud of a date had snuck in, I'd rather Eli handle the greeting.

He swept the flashlight around my room. "It's clear."

The towel was definitely moving downward. "Um, can I put my hands down because if they stay up any longer, this towel is going to fall right off. And I'd prefer that not happen. I've sort of exceeded my embarrassment allotment for the... year." I'd broken rule one. Literally. Not only had I been caught unprepared, but my mistakes had caused the situation.

He shifted the flashlight away from me. "Yeah. Sorry. Just keep your hands where I can see them, Miss Carter."

Of all the deputies to respond to an alarm at my lingerie shop, it had to be the gorgeous one who had just pulled me over and could barely string a complete sentence together whenever I was around him. It was adorable in a way to see him all tongue-tied. But the chances of this guy asking me out were somewhere between zero and negative a thousand.

After tonight, he probably wouldn't even look at me, let alone speak to me. That was a shame because he was one of the good guys. He checked all the boxes.

With my arms crossed in front of me, holding the towel in place, I cleared my throat. "Do you have some sort of report that needs to be filled out? Do I need to sign something saying that it was a false alarm?"

"Nope." He looked at the wall beside me.

Why bother keeping my hands where he could see them? He was making a great effort not to look at me.

"So… can I turn off the alarm and get in the shower?"

His brow furrowed, and he stared at my face. He probably couldn't even say what color my towel was. He hadn't let his gaze drop that low. "Yep. But it's not safe for you to be here… *like that.*"

"Why not?" I didn't react well to being told what to do, or in this case, what not to do. Then I remembered how much Eli hated it when my friend Cami had lived in the back of the photography studio in the same strip mall.

He clenched his jaw. "Someone could break in."

"And you'd show up as soon as they did. I didn't even have time to get in the shower." I walked closer to him, taking out a bit of my frustration on the poor deputy. "I don't plan to live here long if that makes you feel any better."

"It doesn't." Backing toward the door, matching my pace exactly, he shook his head. "Sorry I didn't recognize you at first with that stuff on your face and wearing only a…" He spun around and hurried toward the rear exit. "By the way, the back door wasn't locked."

The heavy door closed with a thud.

After turning off the alarm, I leaned against the door, wishing the floor would swallow me whole.

At least I'd kept my wits about me. I had to find a small victory in the horribly embarrassing situation. Another tiny victory—my towel hadn't fallen off. That was good.

A knock at the door startled me out of my thoughts.

Eli didn't need to see me wearing only a towel a second time, so I leaned close to the door without touching it. I didn't want to leave face mask smear.

"What?"

"I didn't hear the bolt latch." Eli didn't miss much.

I flipped the bolt. "Happy now?"

"Good night."

There wasn't anything good about this night. After all the drama, hunger consumed me, but I had to wash off the stupid face mask before I could go out in public. And put on clothes.

So much for not getting caught with my pants down. I'd been caught with them missing entirely. And it rattled me.

CHAPTER 3

*A*fter washing off my calming mask and putting on something more appropriate than a towel, I called my friend Tessa. "Have you eaten?"

"I thought you were on a date. Oh-no." Tessa gasped. "Was it that bad?"

She was the kind of friend people wrote about in books, the kind who played the sidekick in romantic comedy movies. I probably wouldn't have survived living in this town without her. She made me feel like I belonged.

Tessa was the absolute sweetest person on the planet, possibly because she made sweets all day.

"The jerk showed his true colors before we even ordered." I sighed, irritated all over again. "I drove home, and I'm starved. Want to meet at the barbecue joint?" I didn't have to give more info than that because our town only had one barbecue place, and we ate there often.

"Sure. I'll be there in a few minutes. I need to change out of my jammies."

"You don't need to change. No one will care." I yanked on my tennis shoes and tied the laces.

She laughed. "I care. I haven't yet reached that point of desperation. Yet."

"Desperate. Comfortable. They're all just words. See you there." I hung up, grabbed my purse, and walked out the back door.

Out of habit, I always scanned the area behind the building. I didn't want any surprises. Tonight, I'd already had too many surprises. I circled around the end of the building and stopped.

That dud's truck was in the lot. Why hadn't he left when I told him I wasn't interested? Had he really just been sitting there for a half hour waiting for me to leave?

I stayed in the shadows and watched. Was he in the truck? With my luck, he'd crossed the street to get barbecue, and I'd bump into him again. I didn't want that.

My phone buzzed, and I stepped back to check my messages. If Tessa was texting and I didn't respond, she might worry.

How long are you planning to work tonight?

Was the jerk being stupid or persistent? Either way, I didn't really want him knowing I was living in the back of my shop. Where was Eli when I needed him? He'd been behind the shop only a bit ago.

I tapped out a quick reply. *Stop messaging me. I do not want to go out with you. Ever.* That seemed simple enough for anyone to understand.

The jerk's truck rumbled to life, and he tore out of that parking lot like a spooked cat. Good riddance.

Before I stepped out of the shadows, my phone buzzed again. What did the guy want now?

Nothing. It was from Tessa. *Cami is coming. Harper is working tonight.*

I definitely wouldn't be talking about what happened with the towel incident. Tessa and Eli were cousins, so that made it weird. And Cami was determined to set me up with Eli. Neither of my friends needed to know he'd seen me only in a towel.

Cami's purple goddess turned into the lot just as I was about to cross the street. I glanced both ways, then ran across.

"Sorry about your date. But yay for barbecue. I was craving it." She hopped out. "Maybe I'll take some to Harper when we're done."

"That's just an excuse to go see him."

"Yep." She grinned. "He misses me when he has to work."

"I'm sure he does." I pulled open the door to the restaurant.

The amazing aroma of smoked meat greeted me. Barbecue always made me feel better.

Tessa waved. "I thought you'd beat me here."

"I was slow." Maybe I'd tell them about the jerk in the parking lot; maybe I wouldn't. Right now, I just wanted food.

I fell in line behind them and pushed my tray along.

"What meat would you like?" The guy behind the counter motioned to the array of smoked meats.

"I'll take half a pound of smoked brisket and two ribs." Brisket always made good leftovers, so I didn't worry about ordering too much.

He handed over my food, and I waited while Tessa and Cami got their sides.

The guy repeated his question to the person behind me, and when Eli answered, I glanced around for a rug to crawl under.

For a small town, the restaurant options were pretty good. There were three places. What were the odds he'd end up here? This was the best barbecue around. Of course he was here.

I glanced back, and Eli was staring at the floor.

My assumption was right. He wasn't going to look at me. Ever.

I pushed my tray forward, hoping Cami and Tessa wouldn't notice the man who was well over six feet tall. What were the odds?

Not good.

"Do you want to split a potato salad?" Cami turned, and her face lit up. "Eli Gallagher! What a fun surprise. Do you want to sit with us?"

"No thanks." He didn't look up.

Tessa stepped around me and nudged his arm. "You okay? We really don't mind if you sit with us."

He flashed that Gallagher grin, but it lacked its normal spark. "I'm good. Y'all have fun. I'm going to eat and run."

It didn't seem at all fair that he said lots of words to Tessa but hardly any to me. After tonight, was it any surprise?

Maybe a small nudge—not a full-on assault—would help. Because the man ticked all the boxes maybe it was too soon to give up on my plan of a happily ever after. I just needed to get him on board with my plan.

"He has a town to protect." I slowly lifted my gaze, hoping he wouldn't think I was poking fun.

Dang. Those green eyes accelerated my heart rate.

"Something like that." He pointed ahead. "Y'all are holding up the line."

Tessa and Cami stepped up to pay, but I hung back when Eli touched my arm.

"If he comes back, call it in. I'll circle past a few times during the night."

"How did you know…"

He pinched his lips together a second. "I saw you walking over here."

That was only part of the explanation, but if I prodded

him for more information, Cami and Tessa would know something was up.

Now I knew that when he talked about work, I could get complete sentences. I filed away that tidbit of information. "Thanks, Eli."

He responded with a slight nod. If I'd never seen him around our other friends, I would've called him the strong, silent type, but he was only quiet with me, which made him the strong, shy type. I'd never dated a guy who was shy. Those weren't the guys who asked me out.

I was hoping that would change.

Because apparently Eli was around when I needed him. I just didn't know it.

If he'd seen the guy leave the parking lot, then Eli probably saw me run across the street.

"Sorry about jaywalking."

A real Gallagher grin spread across his face. "Just be sure it doesn't happen again."

I couldn't promise that. Jaywalking was one rule I didn't mind breaking.

After paying for my food, I carried my tray into the dining area. It was emptier than normal for a Thursday night. Cami and Tessa were already seated at one of the long picnic-style tables when I walked up.

Tessa patted the seat beside her. "Sit over here."

I dropped onto the bench beside her and immediately regretted it.

Eli sat two tables away, facing us. Whenever I glanced up, guess who I saw? Dinner was going to be awkward.

"You never answered about the potato salad, so I grabbed one. I can't eat all of it. Help yourself."

I scooped out part of it. "Thanks."

Tessa glanced at Eli, then at me. Her wheels were turning, and I prayed she wouldn't ask me any questions about him.

After downing two slices of brisket, Cami patted the table. "Tell us what happened. The dude had to be awful if you didn't even eat dinner."

"But first, where did you meet the guy?" Tessa pulled a paper towel off the roll in the middle of the table.

"Y'all know that I've been going to look at puppies. Obviously, I'm not going to get one until my house is finished, but whenever they have adoption days, I go look. I can't help myself."

"You should get a kitten." Cami folded a slice of white bread around some moist brisket.

Tessa laughed. "Was the guy at the puppy adoption?"

"Yep. He didn't leave with a dog, so now I'm thinking he just goes to meet women. How low is that?"

"You didn't leave with a dog either." Tessa smirked.

"Very funny." I picked up a rib and pointed it at her. "I go for the puppies, not to meet guys."

"Some guys will do anything to get a date." Cami laughed. "The real question is, what are *you* going to do to get a date?" She hooked a thumb over her shoulder and winked. "Since he won't talk to you, maybe you should talk to him."

"Or maybe I should let the man eat in peace." I didn't want Cami's help to get a date, especially not when Eli was involved. That sort of interference just made everything feel awkward.

The number of singles in our friend group was shrinking rapidly, and all the added pressure of people trying to shove us together had Eli quieter than normal even before tonight. Basically, since Cami's wedding reception, and more precisely since he'd been whapped in the eye with a tail.

I'd tried to warn him about the tail flying directly at his face, but he'd mistaken my waving as flirting… right up until the tail hit him.

But I couldn't stop thinking about her question. What could I do to get a date with Eli?

My last few dates had all been varying degrees of utter disappointment. I kept ending up with guys who had one thing on their mind, and that thought didn't involve a happily ever after. Maybe I needed a different strategy.

Eli was a good guy. More than just the uniform told me that. My gut told me he was interested. Shy, but interested. Maybe a few more nudges would untangle his tongue.

It was worth a shot.

"How long until the house is ready?" Tessa grinned. "You drove by today, didn't you?"

"I go by there almost every day. Contractor said four months." I was eager for my house to be finished, and not just because I was staying in such a tiny space.

I'd scrimped and saved to buy the land, and now, thanks to a few successful years at the store, my dream home was becoming a reality.

The only gaping hole in my perfect plan for a happy forever was a prince.

CHAPTER 4

*E*very morning, I ran through the same routine. After getting dressed, I grabbed coffee and often a doughnut from Tessa's bakery, which happened to be right next door. Too convenient.

When I moved into my house, I planned to eat a healthier breakfast. But for now, the arrangement couldn't have been more perfect. Not only did she serve great coffee and amazing doughnuts, but I liked seeing her every morning.

Glancing around as I pushed open the door to the doughnut shop, I hoped Eli had stopped in for something sweet at the end of his all-night shift. Sadly, he wasn't here.

"Morning." I waved and perched on a barstool at the end of the counter.

Tessa grinned as she raced around. The place was hopping this morning. Not surprising for a Friday.

Firemen just off their shift gathered near the counter, waiting to order. A few cowboys sat at the corner table, talking about the recent cattle auction. And a young woman sat alone at a table, tapping away on her phone.

I loved how this little shop was the gathering place for

new and old in this town.

Tessa set a mug in front of me. "Help yourself to coffee. I'll be back in a bit."

After filling my mug and adding a splash of cream, I returned to my spot at the counter.

Tessa dropped a bag onto the counter and set a to-go cup next to it. "This is for Eli. Will you let him know when he comes in?"

"Sure. Need me to fill the cup?"

"One packet of sugar. No cream." She raced back to take another order. She didn't know about my plan, but she'd given me a great opportunity.

I prepped his coffee, then waited at the counter.

When the door opened, I forced myself not to turn around. I'd let him walk up to the counter, and then I'd make casual conversation.

His arm brushed mine as he grabbed the bag. "Oh, hi." He picked up the cup, and coffee splashed everywhere. On the front of his uniform. All over my pink shirt. On his bag of breakfast. Either the man didn't know his own strength, or I hadn't put the lid on correctly.

"I'm so sorry." I ran to the coffee station and gathered a handful of napkins. I tossed a few onto the floor and started wiping his shirt with the others.

He stood as still as a concrete post. "It's usually empty."

"That's my fault. I tried to be helpful and fill it for you." I dared a peek at his face. "I must not have gotten the lid on correctly."

We'd attracted attention, and several customers watched with amusement as I wiped the front of his uniform.

Clutching the wet bag, he glanced at my wet shirt and stepped back. "It's okay." He walked over to where Tessa was finishing up with a customer. "I spilled my coffee."

He'd taken the blame even though the fault was probably

mine

Her shoulders sagged as she looked over at the spill. "Long night?"

"Yeah." He stared at the empty cup in his hand.

Carrying the mop, she came around the counter. "You working nights all month?"

He nodded. "Four nights on. Two days off. All month. Next month, I won't be a zombie."

"Need me to get you a fresh doughnut?"

"Nah. This is fine."

Tessa cleaned up the floor, then looked at me. "Both of you are a mess. Did y'all throw coffee at each other?"

Eli paled. "No."

Laughing and hoping it sounded natural and not crazed, I wiped the front of my shirt. "That's a better story than what actually happened." I pointed at his shirt. "Need me to wash that for you? I feel awful about this."

Tessa leaned the mop against the wall. "Do you have a clean uniform? You won't have time for laundry."

"I'll figure it out." Moments ago, Eli engaged in conversation. Now he only mumbled.

"Take off that shirt. I'll wash it and have it ready for you when you get up." She treated him more like a little brother than a cousin. How did she plan to run a shop and do laundry?

He stepped away from her. "I'm not taking my shirt off." With his cup in one hand and the food in the other, he walked out the door.

"How long until he realizes he didn't refill his cup?" I dragged the napkins across the counter.

Tessa laughed. "He's not coming back."

"Well, he won't as long as I'm still here. So, I'll see you later. I need to change and run by the house before I open up anyway."

"Catch you later." Tessa picked up the mop and went back behind the counter.

I stepped outside and walked down the sidewalk, pretending not to see the deputy sitting in his SUV in the parking lot.

His door swung open as I entered my store. The poor guy really needed coffee.

* * *

THE LINGERIE BUSINESS was busier than normal even for a Friday, and by the time I closed the doors, I was beyond exhausted. Rather than go out, I changed into my comfy flannel nightshirt. It was long and soft and perfect for when the nights got chillier.

But it wasn't chilly outside. The calendar said it was spring, but the weather thought it was already summer.

I wore this nightshirt because it was long and not see-through. That made it the perfect thing to wear to bed here at the store. I'd been wearing this to bed even before the towel incident.

After eating my leftover brisket and doublechecking all the locks, I flopped on the bed with my romance novel.

Maybe reading about fictional characters would inspire me. I wasn't sure how to get Eli's attention. Correction. I had his attention. I wasn't sure how to get him to ask me out. Making him spill his coffee wasn't the right answer. Clearly.

It was too bad he'd refused to take off his shirt.

A knock sounded at the back door, and I checked the time. Who could it be? Tessa usually messaged before coming over. Cami too. I tossed my book on the bed and unlocked the bolt.

Eli crossed his arms when I opened the door. "You shouldn't open the door for strangers."

"You aren't a stranger." I said it with all the confidence of someone who had just thrown down the winning card in a poker game.

"You had no way of knowing it was me." He didn't even smile.

The man could be incredibly maddening, but he was talking to me, and I wanted to keep the conversation going.

I leaned against the doorframe. "Now see, that feels a little like entrapment."

His brow furrowed. "I just wanted to be sure you weren't having any trouble."

"Want to come in and check for yourself?"

His gaze dropped to the hem of my long nightshirt, but only for a split second. Then he shook his head.

"Thanks for checking on me."

Thanks to Tessa's conversation with Eli, I knew he was working nights all month. Would he check on me often?

If so, I couldn't waste the opportunity.

He tipped his hat. "Night."

I closed the door but didn't turn the bolt. One…two…

"Lock it." Eli had two settings—silent and commanding.

I wasn't sure which I liked better.

Instead of doing as he asked, I yanked the door open. "What if we set up a secret knock? Then I would know it was you. Something like—oh, what's that called?" I rapped my knuckles against the door. Tap, tap, tap, tap, tap. Tap. Tap.

"Shave and a haircut is too obvious. Lots of people knock that way."

"I said something like it. Make something up."

His lips pinched together.

That was my signal to wait. The man was a walking database it seemed. And sorting through all that data took time.

After a few seconds, he knocked out a rhythm on the door. Tap, brief pause, tap, tap tap, tap, tap. Pause. Tap, tap,

tap, silent beat, tap. Pause. Tap tap, brief pause, Tap, tap, tap, tap.

That seemed like an excessive number of taps, but the chance of someone accidentally figuring out our secret knock was close to nil.

"Wow. Okay. You've given some thought to secret knocks. Clearly."

He folded his arms. "That's too long, isn't it? I'll just do the first part. Want to hear it again? Just the beginning."

It meant he'd stay longer.

"Please."

He tapped out the new shorter secret knock. Tap, slight pause, tap, tap, tap, tap, tap. I memorized the number of knocks and where the pause was.

"Will you remember that?"

"Yep. Now I'll know it's you."

A hint of a smile tugged at the corners of his mouth. "Right. Well, I need to get back to it. Don't forget to lock up."

He stayed put as I closed the door.

I knew he was standing out there waiting for the bolt to flip, and I might've counted to three before turning the lock. "Night, Eli."

Even if my new plan ended up unsuccessful, engaging with Eli would be fun.

* * *

SATURDAY NIGHT, I stayed in leggings and a T-shirt long after I would normally have changed into my nightshirt. Just in case.

I scrolled through DIY videos about making wreaths. As soon as the house was finished, I was heading to the craft store and buying oodles of stuff to create the perfect wreath for welcoming guests.

Then I saw posts for the perfect craft room, and another two hours disappeared as I gathered ideas. Perhaps I should add cabinets to one wall in that room. I'd have to talk to the contractor.

Eli's knock echoed in the hall, and I ran to the back door. "Hi."

He tipped his hat. "Evening, Miss Carter. Everything okay here?"

"Better now."

His brow furrowed. "What happened?"

"I was beginning to think you weren't going to stop by."

"Oh." He rubbed his jaw. "I thought maybe something was wrong."

"I'm good. Thanks for checking on me." As much as I didn't like being told I shouldn't live here, I did like seeing him every night.

He gave a quick nod and tipped his hat again. "Stay safe."

I closed the door, flipped the bolt, and pressed my back to the door. Even when Eli was all business, he was swoon worthy.

* * *

SUNDAY NIGHT, I was already in my flannel nightgown when Eli tapped on my back door with his special knock. He didn't make his rounds at the same time every night.

Was he just trying to keep me on my toes?

I opened the door. "Hi."

"Hey."

Stepping back, I pulled the door open a little more. "Quiet night?"

He pulled his hat off his head as he stepped inside. "So far."

If we were going to have a conversation, I'd need to think

of topics. "Have you written any tickets tonight?" I spewed the first thing that popped into my head.

"A couple."

"How long have you been a deputy?"

"Two years."

This conversation was as difficult as ripping open a package of batteries.

"About the other night, usually I lock the door. That guy called just as I got home, and I was mad. I shouldn't have let it distract me."

"True. Please make sure you lock it." He walked back toward the exit. "Well, since everything seems okay here, I'll be on my way."

"Eli, how did you know that guy in the truck was bothering me?"

He kept his back to me a second before turning around. "He'd been peeking in the front window of your store. And then you were slinking along the side of the building right before he tore out of the parking lot. I had a hunch he'd been bothering you."

I glanced at the blinds, uncomfortable at the thought of someone spying on me. "He hasn't messaged me anymore, so I think he got the hint."

"Good. You deserve better than that." He stepped out and set his hat on his head. "Don't forget to lock up."

I flipped the bolt right away. Tonight, I wasn't in the mood to tease him.

* * *

ELI DIDN'T KNOCK on Monday or Tuesday night, and I made notes in my calendar. Knowing when my favorite deputy was on duty seemed like important information.

CHAPTER 5

*W*ednesday night, I'd sat out on my property until late, staring at the stars and dreaming about decorating my finished house. There wouldn't be too many more nights where it would be cool enough to sit outside without sweating.

The house was set back off the road a bit, but the lot was deep. The three acres gave ample space for a large garden, maybe even chickens if I wanted to tackle something new. But those were on my later list.

I would need a fenced area behind the house for a puppy.

Sitting under the stars, I'd lost track of time. Eli had probably already made his rounds at the store, and I'd missed him.

After shoving my camp chair back in the bag and returning it to my trunk, I drove back to the store. The lot was empty and dark. Dark enough that I didn't want to walk around to the back door.

I unlocked the glass doors, then slipped inside, locking the store up tight. I made sure the blinds were completely closed, then went back to my room. Once my jammies were on, I washed my face and tied my hair up in a messy bun.

The disappointment at missing Eli's evening check-in surprised me. It wasn't exactly a routine yet, but I liked our mini chats. He never said much, but seeing him was nice.

I'd even prepared myself with a list of questions to spark at least a bit of conversation. Those questions would keep until tomorrow night.

Nestled under the covers, I picked up my book, and Eli's knock sounded at the back door.

Tossing the covers back, I rolled out of bed. If I answered too quickly, he'd think… he'd think the truth. I was eager to see him.

"Eli, hi. I thought maybe I'd missed your check-in." I made sure to open the door wide enough for him to come in.

"I was by earlier, but your car wasn't here. Did you have a nice evening?" He rubbed at his forehead like he was nervous, then stepped inside.

"It was a nice night. I was out enjoying one of the last cool evenings and the blanket of stars. I didn't mean to be out so late." I wanted to make sure he knew I hadn't been out with anyone else. "You are probably going to tell me that being out at night alone isn't safe."

He slowly bobbed his head. "You'd be right. This area is pretty safe, but you should still be careful."

"Do you have any brothers or sisters?"

His radio beeped, and the dispatcher asked for people to respond to something going on.

"I'll be responding from the strip mall." He backed out the door. "I don't have any siblings. Sorry I can't stay to chat."

I watched as he jumped into his cruiser and left. But I made sure to lock the door.

* * *

ON THURSDAY NIGHT, I read for a while, but then a craving for sweets grabbed me. I didn't want to venture too far because I wanted to be here when Eli knocked. And if I didn't hurry, nothing in town would be open.

I pulled through the drive-thru at the place near the highway and ordered their largest sundae with all the toppings. If I was lucky, I'd get an extra cherry.

When the gal handed it to me and I saw three cherries on top, I knew it would be a good night.

I rushed back, so I could eat my ice cream before it melted.

Eli knocked as I was indulging in my oversized sundae.

"Hiya. It's quiet here tonight. Just me and my ice cream."

"Looks good." His gaze never dropped to my ice cream. It almost sounded like flirting.

I stopped short of offering him a bite. That would be a little too much for Eli.

"I hope your night isn't exciting. Quiet seems safer than exciting."

"Definitely safer. And thanks." He pinched his lips together, then nodded. "I'll see you tomorrow night."

"It's a date."

He hesitated before continuing out the door. "Lock up."

"Yes, sir."

He rolled his eyes, then nodded toward the handle.

"You aren't leaving until I lock it, are you?"

"That's right. As someone once said, *I have a town to protect* and you are part of that town."

Slowly, he was talking more. And I liked our conversations. A lot.

* * *

FRIDAY NIGHT, I slipped out the front door to make a late-night barbecue run.

Eli pulled up in front as I locked the door. "Where are you headed so late?"

I pointed across the street. "I'm hungry. Is it time for your dinner break?"

He glanced at the restaurant. "I wasn't planning to eat until later, but—"

The dispatcher squawked on the radio about something. I didn't understand what the numbers meant, but Eli clearly did.

"Sounds like you have to go."

"Yeah, but maybe another time." Eli shifted into gear.

"I'd like that."

He waved and then headed off to save the world.

CHAPTER 6

On Saturday, I stepped into the store just before closing. "Hi, Issa. How did things go today?"

She worked as a kindergarten teacher during the week and helped me out on Saturdays, which gave me a much-needed break.

"Great. We were busy on and off throughout the day. Oh, and a delivery came in. I set it in the hall."

"Thanks. Must be the new robes I ordered."

"I've been eyeing those lace negligees." She coiled a curl around her finger. "Ryan would love it."

"It would look so good on you."

She nodded. "Since he's been gone so much, I try to plan a nice evening when he gets home."

"Is he out of town again?" I tore the tape on the top of the box.

"Just got home today. It's supposed to calm down once this project is finished."

"You should go. Take that negligee. I'll close up."

"You sure?" She reached for her purse under the counter.

"Absolutely. Go see Ryan." I handed her the lingerie and shooed her out the door.

There was nothing else on my schedule for Saturday night, except hopefully a check-in from Eli, but he didn't start his shift for hours. I unpacked the shipment and counted out the robes before putting them on hangers.

Tessa worked every Saturday, so I often spent the day alone. In the morning, I'd decided on cabinets for the craft room. Having them custom made would have added too much time, so I'd selected premade cabinets the contractor could install and have stained. The room would be amazing.

Then I went to look at puppies. I'd never owned a dog. My desire to have one probably stemmed from the fact that I couldn't have one when I was a kid. My mother couldn't even take care of me. There was no way she could've handled a puppy. My grandma had been allergic to them. My stepmom had hated dogs.

I'd been on my own for ten years, but I'd waited to get a dog until I had a house and a yard.

After moving the last few rompers to a rack with nighties, I arranged the robes by size.

My phone buzzed just as I finished.

"Hello."

"Put on something super cute. I'm sending you an address." Cami giggled. "Haley and Zach are having one of their patio parties, and you need to come."

"I know Haley a little, but I've only met Zach once." I tried to decide if the social gathering would be worth the effort of getting ready. I was pretty comfortable in my leggings. I hadn't exactly dressed up to run errands today.

"Where did you meet Zach?"

"He came in to shop for Haley. Why does it matter?"

A door closed. Then Cami whispered, "If Harper shows up to shop one day, will you tell me?"

"If Harper buys something from my shop, I'm quite sure you'll know. He'd be buying it for you."

Thankfully, my friends had all married good guys. I never worried they'd come in to shop for anyone other than their wives.

"But I mean *before* he gives it to me."

"And spoil his surprise?" Keeping secrets was the hardest part of this job.

"Whatever. Anyway, as I was saying, Zach *Gallagher*—that last name should sound familiar—is having a party. It starts at five."

Gallagher.

Cami had said the magic word, but I couldn't let her know that.

"That's in less than an hour!" I needed time if I wanted to look presentable.

"You're beautiful. You don't need much time to get ready." She laughed. "Sorry I didn't mention it earlier. It just occurred to me."

I kicked the empty box into the corner, then walked into my room. "I might meet you there. We'll see." My casual tone hopefully masked my eagerness.

Flipping through the clothes dangling from the rack that served as my temporary closet, I looked for something fabulous. Something that would render Eli Gallagher talkative. Did an outfit like that even exist?

I ended the call but glanced at my phone when it buzzed. Cami had sent the address.

If Eli was working tonight, he probably wouldn't even be at the party. If I didn't go and he showed up, I'd kick myself.

But I didn't want to go alone, so I called Tessa. "Hiya. Are you going to Haley's tonight?"

I omitted Zach's name altogether, so she wouldn't hear the excitement in my voice when I said the name Gallagher.

"Thinking about it. You?" She sounded tired.

"Sounds fun. Want me to pick you up?"

"No. They live just down the road from me. I'll walk. But don't tell Eli."

"That will be easy because he doesn't talk to me." I tried to sound like I didn't care.

Tessa laughed. She wasn't fooled. "Like you didn't talk the other night in line? Or how he doesn't talk to you when he stops in to check on you every night? You're keeping secrets."

"You know how he is about women living in the strip mall. He's being cautious. And it is a good night for a stroll. I'll see you there." I'd skirted the question for now, but eventually I'd end up telling Tessa about my plan. Just not tonight.

After jumping into the shower—now when I showered, I checked all the locks first—I slipped into a pair of fitted jeans, pulled on a white scoop-neck top, and finished off my casual look with a pair of easy-to-walk-in shoes.

Underneath all that, what I was wearing was incredibly cute, but no one would see that tonight.

If I was too dressed up, Eli would avoid me completely. And Cami would think I was giving into the notion of chasing Eli. I didn't want either of those things. This casual outfit looked more like Cami had dragged me to a party.

I dried my hair, put on a bare minimum of makeup, then tucked my phone and keys in my pocket. Tonight, I wouldn't even take a purse.

One step out the door, I stopped. If it got the least bit cold, I'd hate the walk back. I ran back inside and grabbed my flannel shirt with the lace trim. Practical and cute. With the shirt tied around my waist, I studied the map as I crossed the parking lot.

When the street was clear, I ran across, then glanced back down at the map. I had many talents, and getting lost was one of them. So, even in this small town, I double-checked the map.

A truck rumbled up to the curb, and before looking to see who it was, I slid my keys out of my pocket. The pepper spray key chain was small, but it carried a punch. I shifted my finger into position.

I turned just as Eli rolled down the window.

"You just jaywalk whenever and wherever, don't you?"

The reflective sunglasses blocked my view of his glorious green eyes. It also made it difficult to read his expression.

"You going to give me a ticket?"

He shook his head. "It's your lucky night. I'm off duty. At least for another few hours."

"You cut your sleep short to party?"

"For Zach's brisket, I might cut off an arm."

A truck passed, honking as it went. Of course Cami and Harper would drive by as I was talking to Eli. I'd hear about this later.

"I should get over there." He shifted out of park and started rolling but stopped after only a few feet. "Want a ride?"

I hopped into the passenger seat before he could retract his offer.

For the next two minutes, he didn't say a word. Any chance at conversation was up to me.

If I asked about work, he might actually answer. If I asked a personal question, there was a chance he'd drop me off on the side of the road and head home.

Because I knew he really wanted brisket, I tried the second option. "Where do you live? Now that you aren't living at Harper's."

He pulled to a stop along the curb. I'd underestimated his shyness, and now I'd have to walk again.

He turned off the engine before opening his door. "Cami didn't tell you?"

"If I knew the answer, I would've asked a different question."

After setting his cowboy hat on his head, he grinned. "Right."

I chased after him as he sauntered up the sidewalk. "Are you going to tell me?"

"Nope." He stopped in front of a walkway and pointed at the house. "After you."

Sometimes it was hard to tell if he was being stingy with his words or if he was intentionally trying to frustrate me.

When we made it to the door, I spun around.

Even with those sunglasses on his face, I could read his surprise. "What time are you going to check on me tonight? I want to be ready."

He reached around me and opened the door. "After you."

"You really don't have to worry about me. I can handle myself." I inched closer to him, wanting some sort of reaction.

Looking down at me, he pulled off the glasses. "You going to carry that *tiny* can of pepper spray with you into the shower from now on?"

Dang. The man didn't miss anything. I bet he did know what color my towel was.

* * *

After that complete sentence, one that felt a whole lot like flirting, Eli didn't say another word to me. Forget words, I didn't even get a nod.

For the last hour, he'd stayed at least ten feet away. But he'd looked at me. More than once.

Several of the guys—including Eli—were in the yard, playing Corn Hole. Haley was out there too.

Tessa and I were on the patio, sitting near the firepit and sipping lemonade.

Haley threw her hands in the air. "I win!"

Eli laughed. "Haley, you and Zach must practice every night."

"Right. That's what we do *every* night." Zach shook his head.

Haley poked Eli in the side. "Want to know what we really do every night?"

"No. I don't." He strolled to the porch.

"Roasting time." Haley ran back to the porch.

I leaned closer to Tessa. "Okay so help me with your family tree. Eli is your cousin, and Eli is Zach's cousin."

"Right. But Zach and I aren't cousins. I just know him because he's lived here forever."

"Got it." I watched as Eli hovered on the far edge of the patio.

Haley handed me a long metal skewer. "Jumbo marshmallow or Peep? Which do you want to roast?"

"Roasting a Peep sounds interesting." I stuck a pink Peep on the end of my skewer and hovered it over the firepit.

Tessa stood next to me, roasting a jumbo marshmallow.

When my sweet treat was perfectly toasted, I pulled the skewer back from the fire and tugged the Peep off the end. I promptly dropped it onto the stone wall surrounding the firepit. Too hot.

After licking my fingers to get them to stop burning, I leaned down over the Peep and blew on it, cooling it off before attempting to hold it again. After a few puffs, I had to back away from the flames. Being right next to it had my cheek on fire. Not literally.

Standing upright, I popped the Peep into my mouth.

Between the crunch of the melted sugar and the creaminess of the gooey marshmallow, I was in heaven.

Something made a sizzling sound next to my ear, but before I could figure out what caused the noise, ice-cold liquid cascaded over my hair and down the front of my shirt.

I yelped as the cold permeated my skin. If this was someone's idea of a joke, I didn't think it was funny.

"Oh my gosh, Delaney, are you okay?" Cami ran up next to me.

Tessa propped her hands on her hips. "Eli, what in the world?"

He set the empty pitcher on the table. "Her hair…" Forking his fingers through his hair, he stared at the ground.

I wiped my face, and the pieces started to fit together. "My hair was on fire, wasn't it?"

He glanced at me as he nodded, then dropped his gaze back to the concrete patio. Why was he making such an effort not to look at me? Was my drowned rat look that horrible?

Tessa stepped closer to me and pointed at the front of my shirt. One look, and I understood why Eli was searching out other places to fix his gaze. The pretty things that no one was supposed to see were now visible through the wet white shirt.

I pulled on my flannel and buttoned it all the way to the top. Always prepared.

Eli opened the back door and looked over his shoulder at me. The apology etched on his face spoke louder than any command he'd ever given.

Haley handed me a towel. "I'm so sorry."

"It's okay. Really." When I looked back toward Eli, he was gone.

She shook her head. "Why did he use the lemonade? It's gonna be sticky."

"I'll be all right."

"Eli should've let one of the firemen handle it." Cami laughed. "Maybe you shouldn't tell him that I said that."

"He put the fire out." I needed to thank him for that.

He'd also kind of started one with that smoldering gaze. Or maybe it was just hot near the fire.

"Want me to run you home? Didn't you ride with Eli?" Haley pointed toward the door.

How anyone knew that was beyond me because there wasn't a soul in the front yard when Eli had pulled up. When Cami saw us, I'd been on the sidewalk.

"I don't mind walking." I said a quick goodbye before slipping out the front door.

Hurrying up the street, I kept my keys in my hand, ready for anything.

How long had Eli been gone? Was he on duty yet?

I arrived at Main Street and looked both ways before running across. Not only was I not in the mood to walk all the way to the end of the block for a crosswalk, but I also hoped Eli was on duty and watching. He wouldn't be able to ignore my jaywalking.

Back inside my tiny apartment, I locked the door and turned off the alarm before shedding my wet clothes. I needed a shower. And this time, I carried my keys with me into the bathroom.

CHAPTER 7

*M*uch earlier than I'd intended to be up on a Sunday morning, I knocked at the doughnut shop. Tessa wasn't open yet, but I knew she was inside.

She unlocked the door. "Come in and lock it behind you."

I did as I was told, then perched on my favorite barstool. "Want me to start the coffee?"

"Sure. You're up early. Something bothering you?" Tessa poked her head out of the kitchen. "Trouble with Eli?"

I'd debated about whether to bring up the topic, but now that she had, I was grateful. I needed someone to talk to about this. Keeping secrets was too hard.

"I wish I could read his thoughts."

"Eli? The guy has his thoughts written all over his face." She laughed as she set a pan of glazed doughnuts on the counter. "I did feel bad for him last night."

"Me too." I faced the coffee pot and added water before flipping the switch. "I love Cami, but she cannot hear anything of what I'm about to tell you."

Tessa opened the display case and began loading trays onto the shelves. "My lips are sealed."

"On my way home from the bombed date, Eli pulled me over, and I sort of unloaded on him about guys only wanting one-night stands."

Tessa's mouth fell open.

"It gets worse. When I got back to the shop, I forgot to turn off the alarm. I didn't figure that out until Eli was standing in the store with a gun pointed at me."

"That doesn't make any sense. Why would he point a gun at you?"

"He didn't recognize me in a towel, and I had a mask smeared all over my face because I was about to jump in the shower."

She slapped a hand over her mouth as she laughed. "No wonder he wouldn't sit with us."

"Yeah." I refilled the napkin holders. "If he's interested, why won't he ask me out? I get that he's a bit shy, but he talks to other people. Like you. And Haley. And Cami. Is it really so hard to talk to me?"

"Eli isn't really shy. He just can't form sentences when he's around someone he's attracted to." She lifted her eyebrows and shot me that knowing look. "Occasionally he'll muster up a spurt of courage and rattle off a sentence or two, but it's rare unless you get him talking about something like work."

"Or safety."

Tessa laughed. "Oh yes. I've been lectured on going out alone at night. And the one time I picked up a stranger off the side of the road, Eli came unglued. For me, he repeated all the reasons it was dangerous. Also, he hated it when Cami lived in the back of the photography studio. He'd go by there to check on her."

"Was that the stranger who puked in your car?"

"Yep. I didn't need Eli to explain why it was a bad idea. My car reeked."

"You knew Eli was coming by because he did that with Cami."

"I guessed, but your reaction confirmed my suspicion."

"He's checked on me every night he's worked since the towel incident, but he didn't stop by last night." I looked around the shop. "Anything else I can do?"

"Figure out ways to talk to him. About work. Or you could learn to play video games. He likes those. What do you know about cars? He has a thing for cars."

"Law enforcement. Video games. And cars. Got it."

She closed one case and moved on to filling the next one. "Some of the guys give Eli a hard time about not talking to you. Not nearly as bad as it was during high school, but still. Anyway, because of that, last night was embarrassing for him."

"When I asked if there was anything I could do, I meant is there anything I can do right now. To help you." I tore the napkin that was in my hand. "And people should leave Eli alone."

"Teasing is their way of trying to help him get over it."

"So, what happened before when he wouldn't talk to someone? Does he just have this long list of females he won't speak to?"

Since he was single, I worried there was no solution to his silence.

She shook her head. "Eventually, he gets past it and starts talking. Then he isn't interested anymore."

"Fabulous. That's exactly what I wanted to hear." I reached for the door. "Should I unlock it?"

"Yep. And flip the sign, will you?"

As soon as I turned the sign around, I spotted Eli getting out of his truck.

"Tessa, he's here." I moved away from the door, wondering if I should slip out the back and leave.

45

She set a bag on the counter. "Here's his food. Grab him a coffee cup. I'm going to finish up in the kitchen."

"You're leaving on purpose." I was a little afraid that after one look at me Eli would leave without his coffee.

She grinned. "Guilty. Talk to him."

The door opened, and I slowly turned around. "Good morning."

He gave a small head bob, which was silent Eli's version of a hello.

I didn't move as he walked toward the counter. "I'm not upset about last night. I hadn't even realized I was on fire. Thank you for being a hero and saving my hair. I don't think I'd look good bald."

"Okay." He reached around me and picked up the bag.

The man was maybe ten inches taller than me, but when he was this close, I felt really small. In the best kind of way.

I held out an empty coffee cup. "I figured I'd let you fill it since I'm not good with lids."

As he took the cup out of my hand, he studied my face. "Thanks." He didn't move.

Hopefully, I could find something to say that would get him talking. "Nothing weird happened last night. The store was quiet."

He nodded.

"But you know that. You drove by here during your shift, didn't you?"

The slightest shrug was his version of an answer.

"I jaywalked again when I walked home from the party. It was getting dark, and I figured it was safer to get home faster rather than walk all the way to the corner where there is a clearly marked crosswalk." To any normal person, I sounded like a complete loon.

Eli narrowed his eyes. "You shouldn't do that."

"Which part?"

"Both. No place is completely safe, and cars speed through here at night. They won't be able to stop in time to avoid you."

I leaned in closer. "You make it sound dangerous."

He inhaled, then strode to the coffee pot.

My brain buzzed with attraction. Maybe using words wasn't the best strategy.

Once he'd filled his cup and put the lid on properly, I touched his arm. "Eli?"

He turned around. "What?"

I didn't let his curt reply change my mind. I moved my hand to his chest. "I, uh…"

His gaze stayed glued to my fingers.

When I placed my other hand on his chest, he sucked in a breath.

Inching up on my tiptoes, I questioned the wisdom of what I wanted to do. He might never speak to me again. Or maybe he'd decide he wanted to spend more time with me.

I'd never been good at poker. I was more of an all-in type of player, and that only worked sometimes. Hopefully, this was one of those times.

I slid my hands up his chest and around his neck. As I closed my eyes, he leaned down and captured my mouth with his. Who needed words?

For a man who had trouble talking, he sure could kiss. His lips moved against mine. Hunger and desire crackled in the air, sending tingles dancing on my skin. Was he feeling this too?

If so, why hadn't he wrapped his arms around me?

Crap. Why hadn't I suggested he put his breakfast down before starting this?

Stubble grazed my lips as he turned his head. "Delaney."

Cradling his face, I pressed my lips to his again, wishing I'd also thought to flip the sign to closed.

The bag crinkled as Eli wrapped his arms around me. Then his coffee hit the floor.

He backed up like he'd been slapped. "Tell Tessa I'm sorry about the mess."

"Eli, wait!"

Shaking his head, he rushed out the door.

So much for my great idea.

Technically, for the record, he'd kissed me. And I'd enjoyed every second of kissing him back.

"That was quite a conversation y'all had." Tessa dragged the mop across the floor. "It didn't burn you, did it?"

I ran a finger around my lips. "A little."

"The coffee, Delaney. I was asking if the coffee burned you?" She rolled her eyes.

Glancing down at my coffee-soaked tennis shoes, I stifled a giggle. "Didn't feel a thing."

"I don't believe that for a second. You were too busy feeling *something*. That's why you didn't notice that hot coffee landed on your shoes."

Sighing, I watched his truck pull out of the lot. "I'm bad luck for him when it comes to coffee."

Tessa stepped up next to me. "If it helps, I've never seen Eli do that."

"Kiss someone?"

"Leave like that."

"The way he raced out of here worries me."

Her nose crinkled as she scrunched it up. "Yeah. He might avoid you for a while."

CHAPTER 8

essa was right. I didn't see Eli for several days. A full week. If he drove by at night, he didn't stop to knock. Aside from stalking him—which was way out of my rule-follower comfort zone—there wasn't much I could do about it.

I read a lot and checked on my house at least once a day.

From the outside, the place looked almost finished. Inside, it still needed work. I walked through the master suite. The closets were huge. I'd designed them that way. It would be nice to have the rest of my clothes out of storage and accessible.

After a quick walkthrough, I trudged back out to my car. I'd avoided Tessa's shop this morning, but skipping a stop at her place meant I now craved coffee in the worst way. Would I have time to run down the highway to the truck stop?

As much as I wanted to see him, my stomach soured when I remembered how he'd hurried out the door. Was kissing me really that bad? So much for my grand plan.

I walked out to the end of the driveway where I'd parked. Parking any closer to the house guaranteed nails in my tires.

A truck rumbled past, and I gasped. Eli? The brake lights flickered, but he didn't stop. Did he live out here? Had he seen me?

Following him would be weird. I was already his bad luck charm. I didn't need to add stalker and desperate to the list.

But since he was headed away from town, I was going to Tessa's shop to get coffee. There was a bright side to everything.

One of the best things about my new house was that it was only five minutes from the strip mall. I parked and ran inside the doughnut shop.

The crowd had thinned a little, which was nice because that meant Tessa would have time to chat.

"Missed you this morning. Someone else did too. He sat at that corner table for almost an hour before finally trudging out of here." She set a mug and a cream-filled doughnut in front of me. The woman knew what to give me when the world seemed like it was falling apart.

His actions didn't make sense. Why would he wait for an hour, which made it seem like he wanted to see me, but then drive right on past? Maybe he hadn't seen me after all.

I filled my coffee mug before biting into the doughnut.

Tessa rubbed my shoulder. "I wish I knew what to say."

"Do you think it bothers him that I'm older than he is? He's what… twenty-five?" If I could pinpoint the problem, I'd have a better chance of finding the solution. That was the way planning worked. If there was a problem in Plan A, Plan B was created to fix the problem.

"He's twenty-six, and based on what I saw here the other morning, that's not an issue for him." She smiled. "All kidding aside, no. I don't think that's why he goes silent. It's just the way he is. He's a thinker, and attraction sends his brain into overdrive. A two-year age difference isn't that big a deal."

"Work and safety. I'll focus on those things. Because I

know next to nothing about cars, and I'm all thumbs when it comes to video games." I finished my doughnut. "What if I don't get a chance to talk to him?"

"I'm sure you'll figure something out." She glanced toward the door. "Customers. I'll talk to you later."

"Bye." I hurried back to the store and made sure everything was in proper order before opening.

There had to be a way to talk to Eli.

The other option was to forget about Eli. This whole plan of trying to get his attention made me feel like I was back in high school. The difference was, in high school, I hadn't chased anyone. The guys had chased me. Even back then, they weren't the guys I wanted.

I turned on the lights in the store and flipped the sign to open. If Eli was interested, he could make a move. All my efforts to be around him had only ended up adding stains to my clothes.

One of my regulars walked into the shop. With her colorful track suit and mischievous grin, she looked like trouble. The fun kind.

"Good morning. Lovely day, isn't it?" She walked around the racks, occasionally picking up bra and panty sets. "I always start here and look at all these cute ones before I end up buying an old-lady set." She reached into her oversized purse. "I brought you one of my new books."

"Thank you. It's Tandy, right?"

"You remembered. Don't worry about me. I'll holler if I need something."

"Please do." I set the book on the counter and smiled as a man walked in. "How may I help you?"

"I'm shopping for a friend. She's built about like you are."

A friend? Did she know that? Ugh. Maybe there were no good guys, only bad boys, married men, and silent ones. Now I was on high alert because the built-like-you comment almost always preceded the request to model the merchandise.

Monday was off to a great start.

"What type of lingerie are you wanting to get her?"

He scanned the room, then walked over to a rack of chemises. "Something like this would work. These hug the body, don't they?"

I'd never seen this guy around town. He was well-dressed, and his shoes were expensive. He wasn't a local.

Had he driven to my store so that no one he knew would see him shopping?

"They do. Very flattering."

He picked up a sheer chemise. "I'm not sure what size. Could you—"

Tandy swooped in, and I bit my lip. I'd heard stories about how she could be, but I'd never been witness to it.

"You need someone to try that on? I can do it. I'm about the same size as Ms. Carter. Just a bit more wrinkly. But that won't matter as far as size."

The man's eyes widened as he looked from the chemise to Tandy. "I think a medium will work."

"Fabulous. Glad I could help!" She wiggled her fingers as she strolled to the back of the store.

"Would you like me to wrap that up for you?" I walked to the register.

"Yeah. That'd be great." He laid a credit card on the counter, a card that matched his platinum wedding band. "And I'm going to get one more thing. Could you wrap it separately?"

"Of course." I watched as he scanned tags on the robes and picked up an elegant pink one.

"This is good."

It was a bit odd that he purchased a sheer piece in medium and a floor-length robe in extra-large. He was not one of the good guys.

That settled my dilemma. I could endure a few more coffee spills if it meant Eli would ask me out. Good guys weren't all that common, and I shouldn't give up too easily.

I handed over two wrapped packages and a receipt. "Thank you for shopping with us."

He nodded and glanced toward the back of the store. "Does she work here?"

"Oh no. She's an author who comes in fairly often."

"Oh." The man hurried toward the door, then whipped around. "Which one is which?"

"The ribbon matches what's inside."

"Whew. It would be horrible if I mixed them up."

"Then I hope I got them into the right boxes." I flashed my sweetest smile.

He needed to worry a bit.

* * *

AFTER MY SECOND trip out to the house in one day, I called Tessa. "Hi! Quick question. Eli isn't working tonight, is he?"

"You realize that I'm his cousin and not his secretary, right?" She chuckled.

"If you know, please tell me. I've lost track. Was he in uniform this morning?"

"Yes, he was in uniform this morning."

"Thanks. That means he's off tonight and tomorrow." I didn't want to spend the evening hoping he'd stop by if he wasn't even working.

"Does this mean you have big plans for tonight?"

"Nope. Just trying to figure out his schedule." I parked in front of the store.

"Well, if you aren't busy, you should come over."

"Sounds good. What can I bring?"

"Nothing. Just come whenever." She ended the call.

Spending time at Tessa's was a welcome distraction. I pulled my hair into a ponytail and changed into leggings and a T-shirt. I dressed for comfort because Tessa wouldn't care what I wore.

I grabbed my keys, set the alarm, and drove to her apartment. I didn't feel like walking.

At her door, I knocked as I pushed it open. "It's me."

"Make yourself at home. I'll be out in a minute."

I wandered into the kitchen. "Whatever you have in the oven smells incredible."

"Something I threw together."

Someone knocked at the door, and I peeked down the hall. "Want me to get that?"

"Please."

I pulled open the door.

Eli.

His fitted T-shirt showed off what his uniform didn't. I'd seen him in T-shirts before but never in shorts. It was a treat.

When I finished my not-so-quick survey, I met his gaze. He stared and didn't even give one of his little nod greetings. Or maybe he'd done that when I was looking at other parts of him.

"Hi." I stepped aside and gave him room to walk in. "Want to come in?"

He scrubbed his face. This post-kiss interaction was more awkward than I'd imagined.

"Did you walk here?" He held my gaze.

That question came out of nowhere.

"I drove."

"Good." Without another word, he walked away from the door.

Tessa ran up and leaned out. "Eli!"

He waved without looking back.

This was going to be more difficult than I thought. My gut said Eli was worth it.

Tessa shook her head. "I'm so sorry. That didn't work out like I planned."

"I should've walked over here."

"Then he would have parked out front until you decided to go home." She nodded toward the kitchen. "Let's eat."

"He didn't even come in." I needed a better plan.

"I called him as soon as I got off the phone with you and invited him for dinner. I failed to mention that you were coming too."

"I do think it's cool that you hang out with your cousin. I see my cousins at family reunions like once every ten years."

"We both grew up here. We were born a few months apart—he's six months younger—and we're both only children."

"So y'all basically grew up together."

"We did. My mom worked, so my aunt took care of me. Eli and I were always together. I know he's really embarrassed about spilling coffee on you. Especially after the lemonade incident."

"So far with Eli, it's been one incident after another. The towel incident. The coffee incident. The lemonade incident. And I can't leave off the kissing incident."

"It's funny that he asked if you walked."

"Kinda. The other night I mentioned that I walked home, and he told me I shouldn't do that."

"Sounds exactly like Eli."

"I had a guy almost ask me to model a sheer chemise today. Another customer nixed that idea. But that got me thinking. I like Eli because he isn't the kind of guy who would ask me to model lingerie. Or come into the store and say he's shopping for his mom. I need to do something to get Eli's attention."

"You going to start jaywalking every night when he's on duty?" She set a plate in front of me.

I pointed at her with my fork. "Genius. That's way better than my idea." I didn't need a ticket for speeding anyway.

CHAPTER 9

I scrolled through social media, killing time until I knew Eli's shift had started. The last two days, I'd thought about him often. The look he'd given me right before leaving Haley's party still gave me chills.

Every part of me wanted to be around him. Even if he only nodded and grunted. Kissing was optional. How could I convince him that I was safe?

That was a question for another time. Right now, I had to tackle the seeing him part. Timing would be key in snagging his attention. Tessa's idea seemed like the best place to start. Jaywalking.

A perfectly timed run across the street would spark a conversation or a mini lecture. I was fully prepared for the lecture. Then I'd go get barbecue. Win-win.

I paced on the sidewalk. Traffic was nonexistent. Turtles could've chased each other across the road without fear of being run over.

In theory, it was the perfect time to cross, but I waited for a certain vehicle to come into view. If Eli had taken the back way to the highway, I'd be standing here a while. The highway was part of what he patrolled. I knew that from stories I heard.

He had a talent for pulling over women when they were in tears. Poor guy. I bet not all of them spewed all their problems at him.

I waited a little longer.

The chances of crossing in front of a different deputy were fair to middling, but I'd have to take that risk.

When I spotted a sheriff's vehicle way down the road, I dashed across Main Street. Eli would feel obligated to stop and lecture me.

I walked toward the restaurant at a snail's pace, giving him plenty of time to pull into the lot and stop. But he didn't turn. In fact, he didn't even glance at me as he drove on down the street.

He could've at a least flipped on his siren, so that I could've consoled myself with the idea that he was racing to an emergency. But no. Jaywalking wasn't going to work.

In addition to lots of barbecue, I needed a banana pudding. Maybe two.

Tessa grinned when I walked in. "I figured you'd show up here. Sorry he didn't stop."

"Saw that, did you? I'm going to have to find other ways to talk to him."

"Or you could be patient and wait until he decides to talk to you."

"I'm not liking that approach. Once he gets to that point, he might not be attracted to me anymore. You said—"

"I should never have said anything about that." Tessa sighed. "I'm hungry. Let's order and you can tell me about how the house is coming along."

After we'd paid for our food, she and I headed for the far corner where we could talk without being overheard.

"Tessa, I'm a grown woman who is running across the

street to get a guy's attention. What's wrong with me? Why didn't it work?

Tessa glanced down at her phone and slapped a hand over her mouth as she laughed. "It did work." She slid her phone across the table so I could read the text on the screen.

Tell Delaney it's dangerous to cross in the middle of the street.

"He texted *you*?" I tapped out a message and hit send before Tessa could tell me to stop. *Tell her yourself.*

His reply popped up a second later. *I tried. She won't listen to me.*

Well, crap. That backfired. I'd have to find a different way to get him to talk to me. I just wasn't sure how. Getting pulled over would probably work, but breaking rules— except for jaywalking—made me twitchy.

* * *

On Thursday afternoon, a big shipment arrived, so I didn't go galivanting through the county, trying to get a certain deputy to pull me over. That adventure would have to wait until another night.

I counted items as I pulled them out of the box. Then I hung each one on a rolling rack. It was easier to roll that around the store rather than carry one armload at a time.

Counting super cute rompers, I didn't stop when my phone rang. Once I'd written down all the counts for each size, I picked up the phone.

It started ringing again immediately.

"Hello, Tessa. What's up? I'm surprised you are. It's very late, and don't you start making doughnuts at like four?"

"I *was* asleep. But then Eli called me over and over until I answered. He wants to know why your lights are on so late."

I listened to see if she'd done a group call. "Only the two of us on the line?"

"Yes. I told him I'd call him back."

"Don't call him. Go back to sleep. And I'm sorry."

She yawned. "Good luck."

It was wonderful having a friend who picked up on my thought process even when half asleep.

I unlocked the front door and stepped out onto the sidewalk. The wind gusted, and I crossed my arms as goosebumps erupted on my skin. Except for my car, the lot was empty. Eli wasn't camped in front of the store, checking on me. I stepped back inside and locked the front door.

I wasn't going to make the mistake of leaving a door unlocked again.

An idea struck me just as I picked up a bodysuit. I hurried out onto the back sidewalk just as his SUV passed my door.

The brake lights came on, and he stopped. But he didn't get out.

If he wanted to play games, fine. How could I make him crazy? I hadn't picked up my keys, so I couldn't just launch out on a late-night stroll.

Then I spotted a small rock.

If leaving a door unlocked bothered him, then leaving a door open would definitely get him out of his SUV.

I kicked the rock into the doorjamb and went back inside. The small rock did its job and prevented the door from closing.

Waiting right inside the door, I counted. One... two... three...

Fingers appeared, picked up the rock, then disappeared. The door closed.

I yanked it back open. "Really? You woke up Tessa?"

Eli's gaze danced around. After looking at my face, he focused on the bodysuit in my hand. Then his gaze dropped to the ground. "Everything okay here? I noticed activity as I went by."

"Ten four, good buddy. Everything is a-okay here at the store." My retort had more of an edge than I'd intended.

His shoulders sagged. "I don't talk like that."

"I know you don't. I'm sorry." I tucked the bodysuit behind my back. "Will you come in for a minute? Please." I didn't want him leaving upset with me.

In the most shocking surprise of the week, he nodded. "I can make sure nothing is amiss."

"Thank you. I appreciate that."

He took off his cowboy hat as he walked inside, and I followed him down the hall, watching as his gun belt shifted with each step.

"As you can see, I've been unboxing a shipment. I should be done in about an hour." I stood beside the rolling rack.

The man made a visible effort not to look at all the pretty things. It was completely adorable and made me wonder what thoughts were bouncing around in his head. Unlike Tessa, I didn't have the ability to read his face.

"Good. Well, I'll let you get back to work." He patted his hat against his leg as he turned to go back down the hall.

I stepped in front of him. "Eli, when something at the store doesn't look right, text me. I don't want you to worry."

He rubbed his chin, which only reminded me of how rough his stubble felt against my lips. Were there rules about kissing on duty? I shouldn't try to find out. This all-business conversation was a step in the right direction. Kissing him again might send him running. However, there was no coffee here, nothing to spill.

He didn't move, and I stayed quiet, hoping he'd respond.

Eli played with silence like it was a fidget toy. I tempered my impatience. If he needed time to think about what he wanted to say, I didn't mind waiting.

When his gaze lifted to meet mine, I held my breath.

"I don't have your number." His voice came out in a low rumble.

My heartrate kicked into overdrive, and I grabbed my phone. "Give me yours, and I'll text you."

Only giving him my number meant that I might never hear from him. Having his number could prove helpful. I was following rule one—always be prepared.

If there was an award for the smoothest way to get a woman's number, he deserved it.

He rattled off his digits without hesitation, and I typed the number into my contacts. Then I tapped out a quick text. *Thanks for checking on me.*

Those green eyes sparkled as a smile spread across his face. "If you ever need anything, you can… you know."

That was an invitation to call him. I'd remember that.

"I will. Thanks."

He strode down the short hall and stopped at the door. "Night, Delaney."

"Good night." I closed the door behind him and immediately flipped the bolt.

My phone buzzed in my hand.

He'd sent a thumbs-up.

Eli could say more with fewer than fifty words than any guy I'd ever dated. He kissed better too.

CHAPTER 10

On Friday evening after locking the door and closing the blinds, I walked around the racks and made sure items were where they were supposed to be. Doing this at the end of the day made opening easier in the morning.

Once the store looked spotless and ready for business, I turned off the lights in front and walked back to the bedroom. As I changed out of my work clothes into leggings and a T-shirt, my phone buzzed.

Eli was making use of my number. *Do you have any siblings?*

Two half-sisters. They're quite a bit younger than me. I gave him the concise version, not the full sad story. That wasn't something I shared with many people. Even Tessa had only heard bits and pieces.

I wasn't very close to my sisters. They were ten and twelve years younger than me, and I'd always felt like I was an extra in my dad's second family, his happy one.

Are you on shift tonight? I was pretty sure I knew the answer.

His reply popped up right away. *Yep.*

Be safe. When he worked nights, I didn't sleep as soundly. It wasn't so much that I worried, but every noise woke me.

He sent a thumbs-up.

I slipped on my now-clean tennis shoes, thinking about where I should grab dinner. Having a kitchen again would feel like a luxury.

Why don't you come over? I made meatloaf. Tessa's text was proof that she never rested.

I tapped out an answer as I ran toward the back door. *Sounds delicious. On my way.*

When I arrived, I knocked as I pushed open the door. "Your timing was perfect. I was just thinking about what to eat when you messaged."

"Good. Have a seat. I can't eat all of this by myself. How did last night go?" Poor Tessa had been waiting for an update. Her shop had been too busy this morning for us to talk.

I loaded food onto my plate. "He asked for my number."

Smiling, she lifted her eyebrows. "Has he made use of the number?"

"He texted me a few minutes ago. It's not much, but it's something." I took a bite and sighed. "This is so good."

"Glad you like it. Eli likes you. That I know. Give him time."

All my attempts at pushing the relationship forward hadn't worked out that well. "Yeah. How do you have time to make doughnuts, run the shop, and make dinner?"

"You've just described my entire life. It's easy to do all that when I have nothing else to do."

"Maybe Eli has a friend."

Tessa shook her head. "I like the way things are right now."

While we ate, we chatted about plans for summer, how my house was coming along, and bits of local gossip. After dinner, I helped her clean up before heading back to the store.

My phone rang as I walked in, but I didn't let it distract me from turning off the alarm. "Hello."

"Hi. Delaney. Just calling to check in. We haven't talked in a while." Hearing from my dad was a nice surprise.

I tossed my purse down and flopped across the bed. "I'm good. Business is going well. Work on the house is progressing. How is everyone there?"

"Busy, as you can imagine. Lucy is rehearsing for a ballet performance, and Lacey is involved with art camps. She has a gallery showing at the end of the month."

"Wonderful." I loved that my sisters were happy and doing well. "Have you given any more thought to coming for a visit when the house is finished?"

"I want to. We'll have to see if schedules will allow for it." He sighed. "I miss you, Delaney."

"I miss you too. I'll keep you posted on the house progress. Hopefully, it works out for you to come." If I didn't expect it to happen, then maybe I wouldn't be too disappointed when he said he couldn't make it.

"Well, I'm being paged. I should go. Love you."

"Love you too. Bye, Dad."

Things with my dad weren't perfect, but I knew he loved me. I'd learned to be content with that.

Eli's knock was the perfect distraction.

I pulled open the back door, not hiding my eagerness to see him. "Hi."

He tipped his hat. "Miss Carter."

That little greeting would work its way into my dreams for sure. "How are you?"

"Not bad. Can't really stay to talk, but I wanted to make sure things were quiet around here."

"Uneventful. I was going to do a little reading before bed."

"Anything good?"

"Tandy gave me one of her books."

Eli rolled his eyes. "That woman and her books. I think she asks every man she meets to pose on her covers."

"Every man? I think maybe just the ones who look good without a shirt." It should've occurred to me based on his comment that he'd been asked to pose for a cover. I might've phrased my comment differently.

He kicked at the rock he'd pulled out of the doorway days ago before looking up. "You think so?"

"Absolutely. Have you seen her covers?" I pointed back toward my room. "Let me grab the book."

"No. There's no need. I believe you." He stepped back. "I'll talk to you later."

"Thanks for stopping by."

He nodded. "Thanks for the compliment."

After that conversation, I'd be doing a lot more wondering about how Eli looked without a shirt and a lot less reading.

* * *

THE NEXT NIGHT, just after closing, Eli texted again. *Where did you grow up?*

I stared at the question, wishing he hadn't asked a question that was hard to answer. *The answer is sort of complicated, but I graduated from high school in a suburb of Dallas. My dad and stepmom now live in Colorado.*

Hoping he didn't ask any follow-up questions on that topic, I sent him a text. *Tessa mentioned that y'all grew up together, so I guess you've lived here a while.*

All my life. I won't be making the rounds at the strip mall until late, so I'll just drive by without knocking. That wasn't good news.

Hope work goes well.

He sent a happy face. That was new.

* * *

SUNDAY MORNING, I slept in. It was a rare treat. Usually, my brain wouldn't let me stay asleep that long. The downside was that the doughnut shop was packed. I grabbed a coffee and doughnut to go.

Scrolling through decorating ideas online, I tried to decide what to do with my day. Going to the house was on my agenda, but otherwise, I had nothing to do.

A text from Eli popped up on my screen, and it made me smile. *What do you put in your coffee?*

His random text questions were entertaining.

Cream, no sugar.

Eli texted again. *I'm about to turn into a pumpkin, so I'm crawling into bed, but I'll message later if that's okay.*

I'm enjoying your questions. I watched for a second, waiting for his response. But it never came.

He was probably one of those guys who fell asleep as soon as his head hit the pillow.

Later that evening, he texted as promised. *What's your favorite color?*

I might as well give him the full answer. *Blue. I prefer the shades on the green side of the spectrum more than those on the red side.*

A laughing emoji popped up before his reply. *Very specific. I like blue too. And I like the color of your hair. It's especially beautiful when the light hits the pretty brown.*

How could he send such charming messages and be so limited with words when he was around me?

I sent a heart, then followed up with another text. *I like the way your stubble feels against my lips.*

I'll keep that in mind. Have a good night. Had he wrapped up our text conversation early because of what I'd sent or was this just part of the little dance?

FOR THE NEXT FEW DAYS, Eli messaged me every day. The texts were short, usually just one question. But this ongoing communication made me happy.

CHAPTER 11

*A*s soon as the store closed, I drove out to the house, hoping to catch the contractor before he left.

I parked near the road and hurried up to the house as he walked out the front door. "Hi. I was hoping for a quick update."

"Electricians have been running wires. Sheetrock is going up. I'm thinking another two months. Maybe a little longer."

"That's great news!"

He checked the time. "I have an appointment. Otherwise, I'd walk through with you and answer questions."

"Another time." I said goodbye to the contractor and climbed into my car. With such good news about the house, I felt a little like celebrating, so I drove to the winery down the road and hoped that the restaurant would have a table for one available.

The parking area wasn't too packed, so maybe the place wasn't all that crowded. Or maybe the crowds were on their way. It was Thursday. Lots of people went out on Thursdays, but it didn't hurt to check.

Smiling, I walked up to the hostess's desk. "Hi. I don't

have a reservation, but I was hoping you had a table for one available."

The hostess trailed her finger down a sheet in front of her before holding up one finger. "Let me check on something."

As soon as I nodded, she hurried away to an area blocked by a large stone fireplace. There wasn't a fire in it tonight because the weather was too warm, but it still added to the warm atmosphere.

Cami had gushed about this place, and now I understood why.

When the hostess came into view, she motioned for me to follow her. "The chef has a table in a tucked away corner, and no one is booked here for tonight, so enjoy."

"Are you sure?" It was almost too romantic a spot for me to be sitting by myself.

"Totally. He'll come out and chat with you soon. And Felipe will be your server."

My phone buzzed, and Eli's name on my screen made me smile.

You're building a house?

I loved how he cut straight to his question. I also wondered how he knew. Maybe Tessa had mentioned it.

Not with my own two hands, but yes. Two more months. I can't wait to be out of that little apartment. I know you'll be happy about it too.

Yep.

I imagined him sitting in his truck with that heart-melting Gallagher grin on his face.

I hope you have an easy shift tonight. That was not only being nice, but it also let him know I paid attention to when he worked.

He wasn't the only one who noticed things.

Hope so too. There's been some flagrant jaywalking lately. But I'm investigating.

Here I was at this deliciously romantic table, and I was texting. His messages were the highlight of my evening.

Do I need to turn myself in? I probably looked like a dork grinning at my phone, but since I was back here at the chef's table, no one could see me except the waiter who had stepped around the corner, then hurried away like he'd forgotten something.

Eli replied: *I'll let you know.*

It was as if Eli had one goal in life… to make me wait. Wasn't there a saying… good things come to those who wait?

Hopefully, it was true. And I'd wait.

You know where to find me. I followed the text with a happy face.

He sent a thumbs-up.

I snapped a picture of the centerpiece. *Trying a new place tonight. The place at the winery. I've heard it's good.*

Sorry for interrupting your date.

No date. Just me. I wasn't going to play hard to get.

This time he sent a smiley. *Let me know how it is. I might have to try it.*

I will. As soon as I hit send, I kicked myself for missing the opportunity to send a thumbs-up.

I set my phone on the table, not expecting any more messages from him. He was at work. Or at least he would be in four minutes.

The waiter smiled as he sauntered up to the table. "I didn't want to disturb you. Someone special?" He nodded toward the phone.

"Too early to know." I had high hopes, but we'd only just started having full conversations. Via text. "But his messages were a nice surprise."

"Wonderful. What can I get you to drink?" After getting my drink order, he disappeared around the corner.

"Evening. I'm Jeffrey." A man who looked more like he

71

should be out on a ranch than in a kitchen strolled up to my table. "Welcome to my restaurant."

"I feel a little like I've crashed a party. Thank you for letting me sit at your table."

"We're glad to have you. There's no point in your going hungry when no one was using this table."

"I can't wait to taste the food. My friend Cami raves about this place." I hadn't even glanced at the menu, and I was already salivating. Because of the way the restaurant smelled. Not because of the older but completely hot chef standing next to my chair.

"Any friend of Cami's is a friend of mine." He glanced back toward the kitchen. "Felipe should be back in a moment. Enjoy your evening." After a quick wink, he strode away.

The atmosphere here was nice. Very nice.

* * *

I SPRAWLED out on my bed, stuffed from the incredible meal. Since I'd told Eli I'd give him a report on the place, I picked up my phone. Now was as good a time as any to text him. He was on duty, so I didn't expect a response right away.

Dinner was amazing. I ended up at the chef's table. Highly recommend. I dropped my phone next to my pillow and opened Tandy's book to where I'd left off.

Not even a minute later, my phone buzzed when he responded: *Jeffrey?*

I think maybe that was the chef's name. But I meant that I recommend the restaurant. Best steak I've ever had and the lavender crème brûlée was divine. I waited two minutes before sending another message. *Do you know everyone in this town?*

Nope.

His one-word texts didn't make for great conversation.

I'll stop bothering you so that you can work.

Staring at the phone wasn't going to make him respond any faster. So, I read until I couldn't keep my eyes open any longer

A buzzing sound woke me, which was my own fault because I slept with the phone beside my pillow.

As soon as I read the reason for the buzz, I swallowed back any hint of a complaint.

You aren't a bother, Delaney.

I could almost hear the low rumble of his voice saying it, and it made my knees weak. Before rolling over and going back to sleep, I sent him a smiley face. That didn't do justice to the way his message made me feel, but it would have to do.

Sorry I woke you.

Worth it. At this time of night, honesty was the only option.

Sweet Dreams.

My fingers tapped out a message before my brain could filter it. *You'll probably be in them.*

He sent a winking emoji.

All the teasing he'd endured was completely undeserved. Eli was a master flirter when it came to texting. Sometimes even in person, he pulled off a surprise. Like on the porch. My spine still tingled when I remembered him whispering about carrying my tiny pepper spray into the shower.

I definitely wanted to get to know him better.

CHAPTER 12

*T*he next morning, I showed up at the bakery bright and early. "Good morning."

Tessa wiped her hands on her apron. "Someone is in a good mood."

"Eli and I *talked*"—I gestured air quotes—"last night. Twice. He's been texting all week. He asked about my house. Did you tell him I was building?"

"I did not. Eli doesn't mention you when we hang out. If I bring up the topic, he goes silent. So no, I haven't told him you're building a house."

"He drove by when I was out there one day. Maybe he saw me." I couldn't wait to chat with him again.

Tessa filled a coffee mug. "He called you?"

"Texted. He's much more talkative with his fingers than he is with his tongue." I could feel my cheeks heating. "I'm glad no one else is here yet. That sounds horrible without context."

"Even with context, it's odd." She laughed. "Big plans this evening?"

"I'm going to a puppy adoption. Since the house isn't quite ready, I can't get one yet. But…" I shrugged.

She knew I was eager to move into my new place. "But it doesn't stop you from looking."

"Exactly. I am so ready for a fuzzy friend. And I think having a dog will be good. For safety."

"Unless you get a tiny dog. They aren't much help warding off bad guys."

"Have you met any chihuahuas?" I didn't want that kind of dog. "I'm hoping to get a medium-sized dog. Well, a puppy that will grow into a medium-sized dog. I love the ones that you see on fox hunts. I don't even know what they're called. But I'm going to see if I can find a puppy to adopt. Because those little guys need homes."

"That's sweet." She tapped on her phone.

I made an effort not to look at her screen. "Eli?"

"He hasn't called this morning. Usually, he calls before he gets off so that I can have his breakfast bagged up and ready."

"Is that your way of warning me that he might not be coming?"

"I wasn't subtle enough?" She patted my hand before waving at the firemen walking in. "Morning, guys. What can I get ya?"

While she was busy getting the hungry firefighters their pastries, I headed to the door. Eli wasn't going to stop by, and Tessa was busy.

As I pushed open the door, Joji walked up, a bright smile lighting up her face. "Delaney! How are you this morning?"

She was close to Cami and came into the doughnut shop often. Joji also frequented my store regularly.

"Pretty good. How's the goat farm?"

"Exciting as always. Listen, are you busy tonight? Clint is getting together with Beau, Mad Dog, and Jeffrey. Poker, I think. Anyway, you should come over. I'll be bored otherwise." She nodded toward the counter. "Want to join me for a doughnut?"

I wasn't opposed to having more coffee and eating another doughnut. "Sure."

The invitation had me curious. I knew Joji a little, but not well. So being invited over was unexpected. Joji and Cami, however, were tight as thieves.

My gut said that fact had something to do with the invitation. Knowing Cami's latest quest, I figured it had to do with Eli. But I couldn't figure out the connection.

Eli seemed to know almost everyone in town, so maybe he was friends with Joji. Was she planning to have us both over?

That would be a quiet evening… if he even stayed.

"Sure to which part, hun?" The petite woman held open the door.

"Both."

"Wonderful." She glanced at the parking lot. "Grab that table by the window. My sweetie is going to stop by, and I want to keep an eye out."

"I don't want to intrude."

Laughter bubbled out of her. "You aren't. He won't stay long. When he runs into town on my café days, he stops in. I think it's because he misses me." She tousled her red curls. "He likes me. That's why I married the man."

She made it sound so simple. I could only hope I'd find that kind of love.

* * *

Giving myself a lecture about not getting a puppy before the house was ready, I walked into the pet store. I could only stay a few minutes if I was going to arrive at Joji's on time.

Strolling past the kittens, I headed straight for the dogs. As always, there were very few puppies.

"Are you interested in adopting a dog?" A young woman grinned from a nearby table.

"Very, but I'm waiting until I move out of my tiny place. I can't have a pet there. But I really want a puppy." I continued scanning the cages.

In the very last cage, the one next to the volunteer's table, was the puppy of my dreams. I hurried as my resolve crumbled. How hard would it be to keep a puppy in the store?

Extremely difficult. But if I waited, someone would snatch up my puppy. "But for this little guy, I am going to change my whole plan. I'll find a way to make it work. What paperwork do I have to sign?"

Tessa would give me grief for getting a dog before the house was ready, but the way she laughed whenever I talked about stopping at an adoption made me think she half expected it.

"I'm sorry. This little guy was adopted earlier today." She flashed an apologetic smile.

"But he's here."

Who adopted a dog and left without it?

She put her hand up, blocking the side of her face nearest the cage. "He has an appointment the week after next to be neutered. The dog, not the new owner. The new owner will pick his puppy up after that."

"Poor little guy. I hope you'll be going home with someone amazing." I squatted in front of the cage. "Because you're adorable."

The woman bit her lower lip, then leaned forward. "Just between you and me, the guy definitely qualifies as amazing. Shoot, if he'd asked, I would've gone home with him. Hopped right into the back of his pickup." She winked. "If you know what I mean."

I laughed out of sheer politeness. What did I care that the puppy would have a hot owner? "Thank you for your help."

"Have a nice evening." She walked over to a woman looking at the cats.

After trudging out to the car, I called Tessa. "I found the perfect puppy. He was exactly what I was wanting."

"So you got a dog?" She laughed.

"No." I sniffled for added effect. "Someone already adopted him. They just couldn't take him home until after his surgery. The new owner is probably some pickup-driving hick who only wants the dog for hunting. The poor dog will have to sleep outside and eat stale dog food." There was a chance I was overreacting to not getting the puppy.

"The poor puppy will have such a horrible life." Tessa didn't bother to stifle her giggle. "Need to come over and indulge in ice cream?"

"I would, but Joji invited me over. It was kind of out of the blue, and I'm curious about why she asked. She seems fun though."

"She's awesome. I love her. Have fun." Tessa ended the call without another word.

I stared at the phone. "That was weird. Bye, Tessa. Have a good evening. Maybe I'll see you tomorrow." Talking to myself made me look crazy.

I tossed the phone into the cup holder and headed to Joji's farm. Thankfully, I knew where I was going. When Cami lived in the trailer on the goat farm, Tessa and I sometimes spent evenings there.

After rolling through the gate, I eased up the road toward the main house and sucked in a breath when I saw Eli's truck parked in front of the trailer.

He'd switched places with Cami.

Since he lived here on the goat farm, maybe I'd see him

tonight. My toes tingled at the thought. Then my whole body tingled when I remembered our kiss. Cool it, Carter.

Fanning myself, I walked toward Joji's door. I raised my hand to knock but took an extra second to look back toward the trailer. That's when I noticed the open garage.

A car—no idea what kind—had its hood open, and my favorite deputy was leaning into the engine.

The air out here was definitely warmer.

Had Joji noticed me standing on her porch? I dropped my hand, trying to decide what to do. I could say a quick hello to Eli before going inside, or I could come back outside after going inside and chatting with Joji. But as soon as I knocked, I'd lose the element of surprise.

I tiptoed off the porch, past the chicken coop, and up to the garage. Country tunes rang out from a speaker sitting next to his phone.

Tessa had mentioned that Eli liked cars, but she'd failed to mention that he knew how to work on them.

This was kind of hot. All kinds of hot. Who knew?

"Will you hand me that wrench from the top of the tool chest?" Eli still had his head inside the engine.

Assuming the giant red metal drawer unit was the tool chest, I picked up the tool off the top. It looked like a wrench. "Here."

"Thanks, Delaney." He stuck his hand out, and I laid it in his palm. "Did Boingo leave?"

"Boingo?"

"The goat. He likes to hang around when I'm working on the car."

"I don't see him." I glanced around. "Why? Did you expect him to hand you the tool?"

Eli laughed. "He can't tell a wrench from a hammer. But I figured you'd give me what I needed."

"How'd you know... never mind. Is this yours or are you helping a friend?

"It's mine."

Snapping a picture was oh so tempting. This view would make a great background image for my phone. Or a poster for my wall. The muscles in his arms were visible where his T-shirt stretched over his biceps. And those jeans.

He cursed as metal clanked, and a small piece skittered across the floor.

"I'll get it." I kept my focus on the bolt—or was that part the nut—as I walked around the car. Leaning down, I had to stretch to reach it. "Got it."

He opened his hand.

Standing beside him, I made sure my fingers touched his skin when I placed the nut—pretty sure that was what this was called—in his palm.

He grunted, which I assumed was another version of thank you.

For a full minute the only sounds in the garage were his tools clinking in the engine and my heart thumping. I stayed beside him, looking into the engine.

I couldn't tell one part from the other. Collectively, it was an engine. I'd never bothered to learn about the different parts.

If this was how he spent his off hours, I wanted to learn more about cars. Hopefully, the internet had easy-to-understand training videos I could watch. Of course it did. The internet had everything.

I inched closer to him. "What are you doing?"

"Trying to get it to run." He bumped me with his hip.

"Oh, sorry. I'll get out of your way." I moved away.

He chuckled but didn't stand up. "You weren't in my way."

I eased up beside him again. "So, is that other car yours too?"

"The classic Mustang?" He pulled his head out of the engine and smiled down at me. "That's Joji's."

"There you are! I thought I saw you on my porch." Joji materialized out of nowhere as if her name had beckoned her, and behind her, a goat came running up.

It wasn't that I was unhappy to see Joji, but well, I had forgotten she existed. "Sorry. I saw Eli working and thought I'd say hi."

"Oh! You know each other? That's perfect. I hate to be rude, but I need to run over to the ranch. Out here, there is never a dull moment. I shouldn't be too long." She turned her focus to Eli. "Will you look after my guest? There are snacks on the counter. Help yourself." She petted a dog that trotted up beside her. "Bones, you listen to Eli. Boingo"—she waggled a finger at the goat—"you better behave. I'll be back in a bit."

Eli nodded. "Sure thing."

Pulling keys out of her pocket, she winked. "Have fun!"

Once her truck was out of view, I turned back toward Eli. "I didn't know you lived here."

"Now you do." Looking down at his hands, he gave a small shrug. "Let me get cleaned up a bit, then we can go inside."

I was liking this cozy little scene in the garage with the radio playing, a welcome breeze keeping the temps in check, and Eli showing off some of his talent.

Trailing a finger down his arm, I stepped closer to him. "Don't stop working on my account. I can be quiet while you work or… I can be helpful maybe."

One side of his mouth lifted, resulting in a rather delicious smirk. "Quiet and helpful?"

"Whatever." I treated him to an eyeroll. "Tell me about your car."

He continued wiping his hands. "Delaney, you don't have to—"

"Are you going to make me google the name and read about it?" I slipped my phone out of my back pocket before strolling to the back of the car. "First, I need to see the logo so I can search up what kind of car. Pretty car. It has nice lines."

He crossed his arms and leaned against the wall, watching me.

"Datsun. Never heard of it."

"You really want to know?" He tossed the rag aside.

Nodding, I walked back to him. "I'm interested." Very interested.

The man surely knew that by now.

"They stopped putting the Datsun name on cars before you were born. At least here in the US. This is a 1971 Datsun Z series." He smiled at the car. "It's all original except for aftermarket air conditioning. Manual with an inline six and seventy-seven thousand original miles. It sat in someone's garage for years, and it needs work before there's any hope of getting it on the road."

"Inline six?"

"Six-cylinder. The inline indicates the type of engine. My truck is an eight-cylinder V engine. Called a V-8. The cylinders are arranged in a V-shape with four on each side. This car has all six cylinders in one line."

I hoped I could remember at least half of all that he was telling me. "What are you doing to the car?" I stepped closer to the engine and stuck my head under the hood.

Eli leaned on the car with one arm on each side of me. And for the next little while, he walked me through all the work he'd done and then what was left to be done.

I tried to pay attention even though most of what he

talked about sounded like a foreign language. Also distracting was the fact that he smelled like car grease and sage and citrus. Very masculine. Not the least bit unpleasant. I never thought I'd say that about car grease. When Tennessee Whiskey started playing on the radio, I was in real danger of overheating.

He rested his chin on my shoulder. "Anything else you want to know?"

Plenty, but changing the pace might break the magic spell. "I had no idea you were so good with your hands." Hearing the words out loud, I cringed. That sounded entirely different than the way I'd intended. Heat spread across my cheeks. "I didn't mean—"

He patted my hip. "I know."

Eli was my lesson in patience. We were completely alone with a romantic song playing on the radio, but he showed no inclination of backing me against the wall and kissing me until there was no breath left in my lungs. I might've dreamt about that a time or two.

Instead, he tugged me back before slamming the hood closed. "Let's eat."

Joji had been gone a while, and no part of me thought it was a coincidence that she'd had to leave. Maybe this had been her plan all along.

I liked Joji even more now.

We walked toward the house, and I not-so-inadvertently bumped my hand against his.

He grinned but didn't grab my hand. When we reached the steps to the porch, he motioned for me to go first.

An engine rumbled behind me. "I hope I'm not inter-rupting anything." Joji beamed as she climbed out of her truck.

Eli hovered a hand near the small of my back. "Good timing. We were just about to eat."

I inched back a hair, and the warmth of his hand seeped all the way to my soul. He glanced down at me, that same grin showing up again. If he was interested, why wouldn't he indicate that with more than a grin? It required every last ounce of my patience not to kiss him again.

Inside, a colorful charcuterie board sat on the counter. Meats, cheeses, bread, and crackers were nestled beside sauces and fruits.

"Joji, this looks amazing." I picked up a plate.

Eli pointed at a soft cheese. "Joji makes that goat cheese. It's really good."

After I filled my plate, he piled his with food. When I sat down, he sat next to me.

Joji joined us. "How's business?"

One conversation led to another, and we talked for over an hour. By we, I mean Joji talked, and I talked. Eli only added a word here and there.

* * *

After saying a gushing thank you and goodbye to Joji, I walked out the door with Eli right behind me.

As I walked up to my car, he stuck his hands in his pockets. "I'm glad you stopped by."

"This was fun. I enjoyed hearing about your car."

He nodded and glanced at the garage.

"Well, you have my number." That was obvious.

"I do." He grinned, then opened my door. "Drive safe."

That wasn't exactly how I hoped the evening would end.

With stars twinkling, I drove home, determined to be patient. Eli wasn't exactly demonstrative, but the small things he did spoke volumes. I'd focus on those things and wait for him to contact me.

My phone buzzed as I walked into the store.

The door locked? Eli was thinking about me.

I bolted the door, snapped a pic, and sent it to him. *Safe and secure.*

How long would I have to wait until I heard from him again?

CHAPTER 13

*W*hen I woke up, there was a text message waiting for me, a message longer than typical for Eli. He'd been up late if the timestamp was any indication.

You asked how I knew. I assume you meant how I knew it was you standing in the garage. A few reasons. When you're near me, my nerve endings tingle as if lightning might strike at any moment. Your perfume wraps around me and reminds me of that morning in Tessa's shop. Also, I saw you getting out of your car and staring at my trailer.

How was I supposed to respond to that? I couldn't just leave him on read. This text required a prompt response.

I typed out the first thing that popped into my head. *I'll be smiling all day because of this text.*

He sent a thumbs-up, so he was awake. Was that his only reply? I wanted to toss my phone against the wall. Then little dots showed up as he typed out another message.

I waited as the dots danced. Then they stopped, but I still waited. And waited. Finally, the dots popped up again and soon after a message.

I had fun. Talk to you soon.

As soon as my feet hit the floor, I threw on clothes, pulled my hair into a ponytail, and hightailed it to Tessa's. Moving helped my brain kick into gear, and the pieces started to fit together. When I'd told Tessa I was going to Joji's, she'd known I'd likely see Eli there, but had she known Joji's plan? Hopefully, I'd get a chance to ask, but Saturday mornings were often busy.

When I took a seat at my favorite spot along the counter, Tessa waved. "I set a mug and doughnut there for you."

"How'd you know I'd be coming in?" The crowded room made me curious about how she'd answer.

She winked. "Just a guess."

"Guess, my foot." I filled my mug, then devoured the cream-filled doughnut, hoping my patience outlasted the crowd.

While customers kept Tessa busy, I put in my earbuds and watched videos about people rebuilding Datsuns. After two minutes of the first video, I was even more impressed with Eli.

After a half hour, I started to grow concerned. If there wasn't a lull soon, I wouldn't get a chance to talk to Tessa before it was time to open my store.

She walked up, wiping her hands on her apron. "I probably have about two minutes until more people arrive. I want to hear how it went last night. You had fun?"

"I did. Joji is a hoot. She told me all about her travels."

That part was true. Joji had told me all about her travels and how she fell in love with Clint. But that part of the evening wasn't what had Tessa so curious. I wasn't dumb, but I could act dumb.

Tessa propped her fists on her hips. "Delaney Carter, tell me about Eli."

"He was there."

"And?" She leaned closer, eagerness dancing as twinkles in her eyes. "Did he talk to you?"

"Did you know Joji was going to invite me over and conveniently have to leave?"

She shook her head, grinning. "No, but that sounds like Joji. She's probably been talking to Cami."

"Probably. Anyway, Eli was wrenching on his Datsun Z series. I think that's what it's called. Sweet car." I walked to the coffee station and filled my mug, making her wait. "He told me all about it. The cylinders all in a line. How many miles it has on it. You were a hundred percent right about him talking about cars. He's like a walking database."

"That's Eli. Did anything *happen*?"

If I didn't want her opinion, I might've made her wait longer, but instead, I held up my phone. "I woke up to this message."

Her jaw fell open, and then she beamed. "Yay!"

"That's what I thought until I got to the talk-to-you-soon part."

She handed back my phone. "Be patient with Eli. It sure doesn't seem to me like he's losing interest. I'm guessing he'll be in touch soon."

"You think so? I really hope. We've been texting, but…" I shrugged. I really just wanted him to ask me out.

She nodded, then looked at the door as it opened. "He'll call you soon, I bet."

"Thanks. I need to run. Issa can't work today, so I need to be there." I waved as I ran out the door. Patience. I needed that word tattooed on the back of my hand. Maybe both of them. My plan and patience didn't mesh together all that well. But if this situation required patience, I'd ditch my plan.

* * *

89

THAT AFTERNOON as I was closing the shop, my phone dinged the special notification I'd set for Eli. Yes, I'd turned on my sound. Missing his texts wasn't an option.

You said you wouldn't look good bald. I disagree. Even if all your hair fell out, you'd be beautiful.

I stared at his text a long second before responding. *You know how to make a woman smile.*

Not all of them.

I narrowed my answer. *You know how to make me smile.*

Good. He was probably wearing that signature Gallagher grin. *Mind if I call you later?*

I'd love that. Using the L word was a poor choice, but I typed without thinking, and it wasn't a lie.

I hurried through the closing routine, then drove out to the house before grabbing dinner and heading home. The whole time, my phone was in my pocket or next to me.

Of course, with Eli's impeccable timing, he called just as I stepped out of the shower. With a towel wrapped around me, I answered, trying to sound dressed. "Hey."

"Did I catch you at a bad time?"

"No. This is great." I switched it to speaker and hurriedly put on clothes.

"You know what I like to do in my spare time, at least one thing. What do you like to do?"

I pulled a shirt on, then crawled into bed. "I'm a bit chaotic in my interests. When I'm not living in one room, I spend my free time doing all sorts of stuff that fuels my creative side. I tend to jump from one passion to another. Once I spent a month turning cans into garden art. Then I switched to crocheting. But right now, I can't do any of that. I read and watch videos about all the fun things I'll be able to do in my new craft room."

"Jumping from one passion to another, huh?"

"Crafting passions."

A low chuckle rumbled. "Good to know."

Did Eli have any idea how sexy he was? Even on the phone, he made my heart flutter.

Something shuffled in the background. "What will be your first project?"

"A wreath for the front door." I'd already chosen the design, but I wouldn't buy any supplies until I had ample space to create. "Are you working on the car?"

"Not tonight. Bones and I are out for a walk."

"He's a sweet dog. Do you always take him with you?"

Eli chuckled again. "Every time I walk, he follows me."

"Do you like dogs?" I crossed my fingers, hoping he wouldn't say that he wasn't a fan of dogs.

"I do. Goats and llamas on the other hand, I would not want as pets."

I laughed, picturing Eli trying to reason with a llama. "Can't say I've ever thought about either of those as pets."

"What about you? Dog person?"

"Yes." I didn't gush about how I wanted a puppy. Leaving topics for other conversations wasn't a bad thing.

For the next hour, we chatted. He'd ask questions, and we talked like he'd never been quiet around me.

"I should let you go."

"I really enjoyed this." I preferred in-person interaction because he was easy on the eyes and made my heart go flippity-flop, but I liked this too.

"Night, Delaney."

"Sweet dreams."

"Yes, ma'am."

I'd be hearing that in my dreams tonight.

I slipped out of bed, snapped a picture of my locked door, and sent it to him.

A thumbs-up popped up in response.

* * *

THE NEXT NIGHT my phone rang, and I grabbed it off the nightstand. "Hi."

"Hey. How are you?" Eli used his sexy, rumbly voice.

I'd woken up to a *Good Morning* text from him, which totally made the morning better. Now, we were on the phone again. I'd love it if this pattern continued.

"It was a good day. How about you?"

"Can't complain." Something clinked in the background. "Sorry for the noise. I'm cleaning up after making dinner."

"You cook?"

"Not like Jeffrey, but it's edible." Eli laughed. "With Joji next door, I don't cook much. She likes to feed me, and she's a fabulous cook."

"I miss having a kitchen. But soon. I'm counting the days." I flopped across the bed, settling in for a long conversation.

We talked about family, pets, and favorite Christmas memories.

Then caught up in the delight of the conversation, I said something I immediately wanted to retract. "Tell me about your most embarrassing moment."

He chuckled. "You're going right for the jugular, aren't you?"

If he hadn't been laughing, I would've been more concerned. "We can skip it."

"I was quarterback my senior year. During the pep rally before a big game, I was on stage. Then the head cheerleader hopped on stage to lead everyone in a cheer."

I could already see where this story was headed. "Did you like her?"

"Back then, I thought she was adorable. Anyway, she did her cheer and at the very end, I was supposed to say Go

Cowboys. But she touched my arm, and I just stared at her. Until people started laughing. Then I walked off the stage."

"Aww. Did you ever ask her out?"

"Nah. Later that day, I heard her mocking me with her friends. I might've deserved it, but she didn't seem so cute after that."

"That's awful."

"It was a long time ago. People only bring it up every month or so now." The humor in his voice had an edge to it.

"Downside of living in a small town, huh?"

"Yep. Especially since I stayed in the same place I grew up. Now, what about you?"

"Um." I did not want to tell Eli this story. Why had I opened my big mouth?

"Delaney?"

"I was a freshman. I was not the head cheerleader. I was a nobody. Then after completely humiliating myself and being whispered about in the halls, I wanted to go back to being a nobody."

"That sounds ominous."

"It was horrible. We were on the bleachers for group photos. The school was big enough that you didn't really know everyone, but small enough that the entire school could take a picture together. Somehow, I ended up in the back on the very edge. Just as the photographer told us to say cheese, I toppled off the end. If I'd fallen backward, it wouldn't have mattered. But I went headfirst over the side, and I wanted to die. My dress succumbed to gravity and left me completely exposed."

"Yikes. Most people were probably too busy posing for the picture to notice, right?"

"That was the photo that ended up in the yearbook. The entire school and me, not my face... just my underwear." I sighed. "You can laugh."

"That sounds pretty embarrassing. Did that have any sway on your career choice?"

"Quite possibly. Because what I'd chosen that day was not picture-ready."

"Picture-ready?"

Warmth flooded my face, and I fumbled for an answer.

"Are you blushing?"

"How am I supposed to know? I'm not in front of a mirror." I gathered my wits. "You know what I meant. I don't want you to think…"

"I remember what you told me that night. Please know I'm not like that."

"You sure don't seem to be. It's nice." I stifled a yawn because I didn't want Eli to hear it and suggest we hang up.

But that man didn't miss anything. "You're tired. I'll let you go."

"Eli, thanks for calling tonight."

He was quiet for a few heartbeats. "Talk to you tomorrow."

Now I had something to look forward to.

* * *

THE NEXT MORNING I woke up to another text from Eli. *You're on my mind a lot*. That night, he called again.

But on the fourth day, after waking up to a *good morning* text from Eli, I hadn't heard from him at all. When the sun dropped below the horizon and I hadn't heard from him, I opted to send him a quick message.

I hope you had a good day. I refused to hop on the worry train. There were other explanations for the missed call that didn't involve police shootouts.

A couple of minutes later he replied: *You busy?*

I'm almost through my pile of books. The store is all in order, and Tessa is asleep, so no, I'm not busy.

The Eli knock sounded at my back door. I almost tripped running down the hall.

"Hi."

He scrubbed his jaw, exhaustion evident in the lines on his face. "Hey. I was going to grab some barbecue."

"I'll grab my purse."

"And shoes?" For the first time since I'd opened the door, he smiled.

"If you insist." I hollered back as I walked into my room.

As fast as I could, I threw on shoes, then looked down at my leggings and T-shirt.

"You look fine." Eli could apparently see through walls.

I poked my head out the door. "Were you spying on me?"

"You're beautiful, Delaney. And I'm hungry."

"Don't become a motivational speaker." I swung my purse onto my shoulder and grabbed his hand. "I'm ready."

He squeezed my fingers. "You texted me as I pulled out of the station. Good timing."

"Bad day, huh?"

He nodded as he pulled open the truck door for me. "I might be a bit quiet tonight."

I hopped into the truck, then squeezed his hand. "I'm perfectly okay with that."

His lingering gaze nearly set my clothes on fire. Whatever it was he wasn't saying with words had me swooning.

Funny thing was, the urge to kiss him didn't have my fingers itching. I wanted to hold him, to wrap my arms around his middle, rest my head on his chest, and chase away the dark clouds.

CHAPTER 14

I chatted during most of dinner. Eli stayed quiet. But this was a different kind of quiet. He didn't talk about whatever had happened that made it a rough day, and I didn't ask. Nothing I could say would make it better, but I could be a bubbly distraction. And I gave it my all.

After telling him all about the progress on the house, Eli got to hear about my string of bad dates, which I realized was probably a mistake when he asked for the guys' names. Thankfully, when I rolled my eyes, he smiled, not a full Gallagher grin but even a small smile was a treat.

Then he walked me to my door.

After unlocking it, I turned to face him instead of opening it. "I'm sorry about whatever happened today."

He nodded and stepped closer. "Thank you for not asking me to talk about it."

I gave into impulse and wrapped my arms around his waist.

He pressed a hand to my back, and the other threaded in my hair. Pulled tight against him, I closed my eyes, wanting this moment to last a long time.

When he pulled away, he rubbed my arm. "I needed that."

"Night, Eli." I went through the routine of locking the door and sending him a picture.

This time his reply surprised me. *If you need me, call. No matter what time.*

I sent a heart because I was so choked up, I couldn't even text words.

* * *

THE NEXT MORNING, I woke up smiling. I wasn't even sure how to label how things were with Eli, but one thing was unquestionable. I liked being with him.

I rolled out of bed, eager to tell Tessa about last night. If I arrived early enough, the crowds wouldn't be too bad since it was a Sunday morning. If I waited, then it would be chaos.

After changing out of my jammies, I checked my phone, then fell back across the bed as I read the message from Eli.

I'm rebuilding the carburetor Saturday if you want to watch... or help. Being quiet isn't required.

Yes, please. I for sure wanted to watch, and helping might be fun too. *What time? I can come over after the shop closes at 4.*

4:30.

Perfect. I harbored a hope that we might end up at a restaurant together after we were done working on the car. And I'd be sure to dab a little perfume on my pulse points to keep that kiss in his thoughts.

I ran next door, grateful for the empty shop. "Hey. No customers yet?"

Tessa grabbed a mug off the shelf behind the counter. "Had a few people when I opened. How are you? You seem very chipper for this time of the morning."

"Eli showed up last night. He'd had a rough day at work and stopped by to see if I wanted to grab dinner."

Her eyebrows lifted, but she stayed silent.

"He didn't talk much. Mostly I talked to him about the progress on the house. I think he didn't want to be alone."

Tessa shook her head. "He knows he can call me whenever. His parents live ten minutes from here. And his granddad is only twenty minutes away. It wasn't that he didn't want to be alone. He wanted to be with *you*."

"I think he does. He sent me this." I showed her the most recent message. "He invited me to help him rebuild his carburetor." My cheeks would likely ache from smiling, but I couldn't help it. Every time I read the text, a new wave of happiness washed over me. "I'm not sure that qualifies as anything like a date, but I'm excited."

She blinked. "He asked you to work on his car?"

"It's unconventional, I know. He said I could watch or help."

She grabbed a rag and wiped down the counter.

"What? Don't give me that look and not say anything." I glanced toward the door, hoping she could spill the beans before someone walked to the counter.

"That's his baby. Asking you to help is…"

"Say it."

"Atypical. Just like I'd never seen Eli kiss someone before breakfast in my shop. I've never heard of him asking a woman to hang out while he worked on his car. I hesitated to tell you because…" She shrugged.

"Because you don't want me to get my hopes up in case it all comes crashing down."

"Yeah. Not that I think it will. It's obvious he likes you."

"But now that he's talking a little more, you wonder if he's going to follow his pattern."

"No, I don't think he will. Really." Tessa's nose crinkled when she scrunched it up. "The thought has crossed my mind."

The woman was as honest as the summer day was long.

I downed the rest of my coffee. "That thought has set up camp in my head. And installed a neon sign."

People walked in, and our conversation came to an end.

"I'll talk to you later."

"Keep me posted." She waved as I ran out the door.

While one side of my brain pleaded that I proceed with caution, the other side shoved all the chips to the center of the table.

I wasn't sure how this would play out, but I was all in.

* * *

ON SATURDAY, after flipping the bolt on the front door and closing the blinds, I ran back to my room to change. I'd spent days thinking about what to wear. Something casual enough so that I didn't look out of place working on a car, but something cute enough that he'd want to invite me over again.

I wasn't too worried about that second part. He'd called every night. Sometimes we talked for more than an hour; other times, we only chatted for a few minutes.

Staring at my clothes, I tried to think through how the day might go. Considering the entire engine was covered in grease, I expected that the carburetor was also. Having a change of clothes in the car was a must if I wanted to be prepared for anything.

Why was it so hard to decide what to wear? I yanked on a pair of shorts, then flipped through shirts, waffling on whether a tank top or T-shirt would be better.

My phone buzzed, and I held my breath as I read the first part of Eli's message. *Change of plans…*

Was he canceling? I swiped to read the rest of the text.

Turns out they shipped me the wrong carburetor kit, so we

won't be fixing it today. You up for a horseback ride? If so, slip on your jeans and boots and I'll be there at 4:30 to pick you up.

Sounds fun, but I've never been horseback riding before. I danced a small jig before slipping off my shorts and pulling on fitted jeans.

My turquoise boots had been sorely neglected because I hadn't been dancing in ages, and other than that, I had little reason to wear them.

Every two seconds, I glanced at the phone, waiting for Eli to reply.

At twelve minutes after four, he knocked at the back door. I pulled on my second boot and ran to answer it.

Eli grinned. "Hey. No hurry. I'm here a little early." His gaze drifted downward, then snapped back up. "Nice boots."

"Come on in. I need to grab one more thing." I ran back to my room.

He stood in the hallway outside my door. "Thanks for being flexible."

"Thanks for asking me out." Tying my lace-trimmed flannel around my waist, I stepped out of my room.

That amazing Gallagher grin spread across his face. "Ready?"

"Think this tank top is okay or should I change into a T-shirt or something?" Standing in the bathroom doorway, I stared at my reflection in the small mirror above the sink.

"You're perfect." He met my gaze in the mirror.

I gave an eye roll and shook my head, hoping that he couldn't see the true effect his words had on me. My heart was thumping. My palms were sweating, and a blush spread across my cheeks.

He probably noticed that.

"For someone with a tiny allotment of daily words, you use them wisely."

Still grinning, he stuck his hands in his pockets. I wasn't

sure what had shifted by hanging out together while he worked on his car, but something had. And it was wonderful.

I picked up my purse, then dropped it again. "I think maybe I'll just take my keys and phone."

"That works."

I rubbed his back as I passed him, headed to the door. "I can't wait until I'm out of this place."

"How much longer?" He reached around me and pulled the door open.

Before taking a step, I breathed in that intoxicating scent of sage and citrus. "They're thinking two months. Which was the same thing he said a few weeks ago, so we'll see."

He grunted.

I knew he wouldn't like that answer. But to his credit, he didn't say anything else.

He opened the passenger door, and I climbed in. "Eli, do I get a raincheck on the carburetor rebuild?"

My question danced twinkles in his green eyes.

"Yes, ma'am."

Whatever this was, I was loving every minute of it.

CHAPTER 15

*E*li jumped out and ran around to the passenger side. He pulled open the door, and the delight on his face made me want to jump into his arms and kiss him. But I didn't.

"You can leave your keys in the truck. No one will bother them."

"Okay." I stepped out of the truck and scanned the rugged landscape.

Up the hill, a white stone house stood, and on the other side of it were trees, not tall, but dense and thick with leaves. The red barn in front of us looked like something that should've been on a postcard.

"This is beautiful. Where are we?" I spun in a circle, taking in the amazing view.

"This is my granddad's place. I come out and ride sometimes. And occasionally I come out here just to visit, and he beats me at chess." He slammed the door closed, then clasped my hand. "Come on. The horses might be ready. I called Mario to let him know we were coming."

"Mario?"

"He takes care of stuff out here. Granddad isn't in poor health, but he isn't young anymore. Mario handles the horses." Eli slid the barn door open and never once let go of my hand.

"Eli, you're here! I have the horses ready." A man with dark curly hair and a full beard smiled.

"Thanks so much, Mario." Eli shook the man's hand, then nodded toward me. "This is Delaney."

"Howdy, miss. Nice to meet you. Can't say as I've ever had to saddle up two horses before, but Sugar is all ready for you to ride." He tipped his hat. "Eli, when y'all get back, just shoot me a text. I'll get these two wiped down and put away."

"I owe you, Mario."

This outgoing Eli was the one who chatted with friends and tossed bean bags with Haley and Zach. With me, he was no longer the stoic, silent Eli. Now he was the slightly less quiet, cheerful Eli. And I liked this guy.

"I'll remember that." Mario whistled as he walked away.

Eli squeezed my hand. "Wait here a sec. I forgot something in the truck."

I slipped my phone out of my pocket and snapped a photo. Tessa had to see this place. Or maybe she already had. I'd definitely be asking her about it later.

A door opened in the back of the barn, and I crossed my arms, feeling like I didn't belong and wondering who I was about to meet.

"Well, hello there." A man with salt-and-pepper hair—more salt than pepper—sauntered toward me.

It wasn't hard to tell he was related to Eli and Zach. This had to be the Gallagher granddad. Vivid green eyes sparkled, and that smile had more wrinkles around it, but it looked very much like Eli's grin.

"When Mario said he was saddling two horses, I wandered down to check on a few things. Really I just wanted to see what Eli was up to." He walked to a stall and stroked the nose of a dark brown horse.

"Are you going to ride with us?"

He shook his head. "But it's a good day for a ride. Not too hot yet. Did he say which horse they saddled for you?"

"Sugar."

"Sweet." He grinned and raised an eyebrow, as if he was waiting for me to laugh.

It was easy to laugh. I liked this guy. "I hope she is. I've never ridden before."

"She'll be good to you. I'm guessing Eli will be riding Cream."

"He didn't say." I pointed to the horse vying for his attention. "What's his name?"

"Coffee."

I slapped a hand over my mouth because guffawing wasn't exactly attractive.

"I hope you aren't telling stories about me. It's too soon for that." Eli pressed a hand to the small of my back. "Delaney, this is my granddad, Matthew Gallagher. Granddad, this is Delaney."

"Very pleased to meet you." He tipped his hat. "Y'all have a nice time." He rubbed the horse once more before walking out the door.

"Your granddad is so sweet." I turned to face Eli.

He patted the bag hanging off his shoulder. "I brought food along in case we get hungry. And a blanket."

Who knew that Eli was such a romantic?

"You packed us a picnic?"

He nodded and laced his fingers with mine. "I picked up sandwiches for us to eat after we finished up on the car, but when I realized the rebuilding wasn't happening today, I scrambled to come up with something else to do. I hope this is okay."

Grinning, I bumped his shoulder. "It's kind of perfect."

"Let's ride." He led me through the side door of the barn out to where two horses were tied to a wooden fence.

"Let me guess. The white one is Sugar."

"Bingo. That one is Cream because Sugar likes to follow him around."

"Makes perfect sense." I patted Sugar on the nose. "Hello."

After putting the stuff he'd brought into a saddle bag, Eli pointed to a small step. "Hop on the mounting block, and I'll help you up."

This was the part that made me the most nervous. Not true. The whole part about being on a horse made me nervous.

I nodded and stepped up.

He put his hands on my hips. "You want to keep your hips pointed this way." He tapped my left hip. "Put this foot into the stirrup."

Warmth spread across my back as he joined me on the mounting block. "Put your hand here on the saddle, then push up and swing your other leg over. I'll be right here if you need me."

I sucked in a deep breath, then pushed up like he'd explained. A second later, I was sitting in the saddle. "Whoa. I'm on a horse."

"You mounted like you've done this a lot." He showed me how to hold the reins, then stepped back onto the ground. "Sit tight."

It wasn't like I was going to go trotting away. At least not on purpose.

He swung up onto his horse like a cowboy about to ride into the sunset. This was a side of Eli I hadn't expected. He wore a cowboy hat and boots on the job because that was part of the uniform, but there was more cowboy in him than I'd realized.

He gathered his reins and adjusted his ball cap.

Sugar took a step, and I yelped. "How do I make her stop?"

Eli rode up beside me. "She's just shifting. Let me give you a quick lesson in how to move."

He explained and demonstrated how to get my horse to go where I wanted her to go. Completely out of my element, I gave him my full attention. Right now, he didn't have any trouble with words. He was fully in his element, and I loved this shift.

"Ready?" He lifted his eyebrows.

"As I'll ever be." When Cream started down the trail, which was really just a line where the grass was matted a bit, I nudged Sugar's sides. "Okay, girl, follow Cream."

And she did. It was less nerve-racking than I'd imagined.

Birds sang as we rode. Sunlight dappled the ground as we meandered through trees and alongside a stream. Then we cut back uphill and into an open meadow. Wildflowers danced in the breeze.

"Eli, this is beautiful."

He pointed toward a large oak tree. "Over there is a good place to stop."

After surprising a jackrabbit and sending squirrels running for cover, we stopped near a large oak tree.

"This tree must be hundreds of years old." I wasn't an expert on trees, but one with a trunk that size had been around a while.

"You're probably right. I bet he could tell some stories." Eli swung off his horse, then walked up beside me. "You'll get down doing basically everything in reverse."

I nodded. Praying I wouldn't land on my butt, I swung my leg over the horse and hovered with my stomach across the saddle.

Eli patted my left leg. "Pull this foot out of the stirrup, then ease down."

He'd touched me more during the instruction for horse-back riding than he had in all the time I'd known him… with the exception of the doughnut shop kiss, but I initiated that. Maybe I needed to ask him to teach me CPR.

Once my feet were on the ground, Eli strode back to his horse and emptied the saddle bags. He spread a blanket on the ground before opening a small soft-sided cooler. "I asked Tessa if you had any food allergies or dislikes. She said you didn't like raisins, so I made sure they didn't put any on your sandwich." He delivered the statement with a straight face, but the twinkle in his eye gave away his attempt at humor.

I laughed. "You're funny like your granddad."

"I hope to be when I grow up."

That was funny because looking at Eli there was no question that he was a fully grown man.

I sat down beside him on the blanket and unwrapped the sandwich. "Where did you get this? This looks amazing." The word sandwiches conjured up an image of peanut butter and jelly or a thin slice of ham stacked with cheese. This sandwich looked fresh from a deli.

"There is a shop in one of the small towns near Stadtburg. Gourmet food store with a deli counter in the back." He handed me a bottle of water. "I hope water is okay."

"It's great."

He wolfed down his food, then leaned back on an elbow as he drank his water.

A hundred questions bounced in my head, but one begged to be asked more than the others.

"What changed, Eli?"

We'd texted back and forth, but after spending that night working on his car, he was this charming, flirty cowboy. And while I loved it, I wondered if his interest was going to start waning. That had been his pattern.

He stretched out on his back and looked up into the trees. "You asked about my car."

"That's it? Really? I heard that when you start talking to someone you lose interest." I kept my focus on my sandwich because he was freer with his words when I wasn't staring at him.

He trailed a finger down my arm. "Tessa has been giving you the scoop, huh?"

"She has."

"That has been true. For a few reasons. Some girls—women—are way more interesting *before* you have a conversation with them. With others, I realized the butterflies in my stomach were only there because I was nervous. I'd confused attraction with my fear of being awkward."

I dropped my hand to the blanket, making it accessible.

In his never-miss-anything way, he caught my hint and laced his fingers with mine. "With you, there are always butterflies. But you don't make me feel awkward. Not anymore."

I glanced at him, pinching my lips together to keep my smile from ripping open my face.

He squeezed my hand. "You don't look at me with impatience and act like I'm slow when I'm trying to think."

I laid down on my side, facing him. "I'm sorry I tried to hurry you in the doughnut shop."

He shook his head before shifting so that he faced me. "Don't be. I didn't leave because I felt rushed, Delaney. I left because I felt stupid for dumping coffee on you. Again."

"I probably should have warned you so you could put your coffee down."

Brushing a knuckle along my cheek, he leaned closer. "No *coffee* here."

His fingers threaded in my hair, and he pulled me to him. His lips were as soft as his arms were strong. There was no hesitation. Tenderly, he danced his lips on mine. He hadn't shaved, and the stubble burned my lips in a satisfying way.

I leaned in closer. His hand shifted out of my hair and slipped around my waist. The kiss intensified as he rolled onto his back, landing me on top of him. And it was a good thing I was lying down because my knees could not have handled this.

For several more minutes, he kissed me, holding me tight against his chest.

I giggled when he broke away. "First, wow. And is that why you rode Cream and left Coffee in the barn?"

Chuckling, he kissed me again. "Yep."

I pressed a kiss to his stubble. "You didn't shave."

"You said you liked the way it felt on your lips."

"I do." I rested my head on his chest and watched a butterfly flitting from flower to flower.

Several seconds ticked by as we lay on the blanket.

Patting his chest, I thought back to our other kiss.

"Penny for your thoughts." He trailed a finger across my back up and down, then back up again.

That question was gold coming from a man who kept so many thoughts to himself.

"The last time we kissed…" I wasn't sure how to word my observation without making it sound like I was disappointed. I wasn't. "I guess I'm trying to say that today you are softer. I don't mean squishy or anything bad." I patted his chest again. "You know what? Just forget I opened my mouth."

Laughing, he rolled me onto my back and hovered over me. "I was wearing body armor. And you pierced right through it."

"Oh. Well, for the record"—I ran a hand down the front of his shirt—"I prefer this."

He kissed me again, and I forgot all about sandwiches, oak trees, and horses.

Long before I was ready to end our perfect little picnic, he stood. "We should get going. I want to be back before dark."

He had everything packed up in a matter of minutes. Then, in a not-so-graceful way, I managed to get back up on my horse.

And instead of walking over to Cream, Eli looked up at me. "It won't even be dark by the time we get back. And I'm really enjoying myself."

"Me too."

"I was thinking maybe dessert and dancing… if you like that idea."

I leaned down, intending to kiss him in answer to his question, but my plan went awry. I slid right out of the saddle, but my left foot stayed in the stirrup.

"Whoa!" Eli caught me around the waist.

I couldn't stop laughing long enough to respond. And I didn't even want to think about how ridiculous I looked hanging off the side of a horse. If I wanted to impress him with gracefulness, this was not the way to do it.

"Work your foot loose." Eli acted like it wasn't any big deal to hold me off the ground while I wriggled my boot free.

Once my feet landed in the dirt, I dropped my head to his chest. "I did not mean for that to happen. I'm glad you're so strong."

He wrapped his arms around me. "What did you want to happen?"

"This." I inched up and brushed my lips on his. "I'm not ready for the date to be over."

"Then let's get you back up onto that horse so we can go."

He kissed the tip of my nose. "It would be too easy to lose track of time if I start kissing you again."

The man oozed charm, and I was smitten.

Following his instructions, I hopped back into the saddle. Hopped made it sound smooth and effortless. In reality, it was difficult and clunky.

He patted my leg. "I have a small surprise for dessert. We'll pick it up and eat at my place."

His surprises were going to spoil me.

"Can't wait."

Sugar followed Cream all the way back to the barn, and when we arrived, he helped me down, keeping his arms around me after my feet were on the ground. "I hadn't planned the dancing part. That was a spur of the moment suggestion. You'll have to be a little patient with me. I haven't been dancing in a while."

"I'm just happy to get more time with you." I meant every word.

He could step on my feet all night, and I wouldn't care as long as he kept sweet-talking me like this.

We loaded into his truck, and once we hit the main road, Eli reached across the cab and clasped my hand. "Thanks for being patient with me. Texting and talking on the phone and getting to know you helped me be much less nervous today."

"It's been amazing. I can't believe you pulled all this together."

He shrugged. "When the car plan fell apart, I figured I'd share something else I enjoy with you."

"I loved it. Tell your granddad that it was a pleasure meeting him. And Mario."

We rode along in silence, the comfortable, blissful silence shared by friends.

I gasped when he parked outside the restaurant at the winery.

Eli swung his door open. "I'll be half a sec."

"Okay."

As soon as the door closed, I shot off a text to Tessa. She was probably still awake. *Tonight has been AMAZING. I'll tell you all about it in the morning.*

Tessa texted: *Yay! So happy he finally started talking.*

Eli opened the door and handed over a bag. "Two lavender crème brûlées to go."

This date just kept getting better and better.

* * *

AFTER HOURS OF DANCING, we strolled to my back door well past midnight.

Eli backed me against the door. "I've never had such a good time on a date."

"I was about to say the same thing."

"My shift starts early, so I need to go, but I'll call you after work." Instead of walking away, he inched closer. "But first, this."

His lips pressed to mine, and his fingers threaded into my hair. Just like on the dance floor, he took the lead, and I enjoyed every second. Kisses that began with explosive passion ended with an alluring gentleness.

Enjoying the tingle of his stubble, I ran my hand down the front of his shirt. "*This* is my new favorite word."

He chuckled. "Night, Delaney." As he stepped back, he pulled me to his chest, then opened the door. "Once the door is locked, I'll go. I really need to go."

Feeling a smile tugging at my cheeks, I slipped inside and locked the door.

With my back pressed to it, I sighed. "Wow." Good things did come to those who waited.

CHAPTER 16

Bright and early, I stuffed napkin holders and made coffee, helping Tessa get ready to open her shop. "I knew Eli was good-looking, and I guessed he was a little charming. But he has upped the charm all week, and yesterday's date blew me away."

She grinned. "I'm happy for you. He really is a great guy."

"He remembered that I loved one of the desserts at that fancy place up the road and called in an order. Or texted because I never saw him on the phone. Then we went to his house to eat."

"You went to his place?" She lifted an eyebrow, but her smirk gave away the teasing.

"Don't give me that look. When we were there, Eli wouldn't come within five feet of me." I thought back to the night I'd unloaded on him about men with one thing on their mind.

"And that sounds like the Eli I know." Tessa bit her bottom lip, which she did when she was tempted to do something she shouldn't.

I leaned on the counter. "Tell me."

"He took a date to prom. I think he let someone set him up on a double date. They danced once, and you could've fit the entire band between them when they were dancing. Eli had his arms almost straight." She tapped a finger to her lips. "Please don't tell him I told you that story."

"Well, he didn't dance that way last night."

Tessa looked at her phone. "Eli is on his way. You want to write a note on his napkin?"

"From your tone, I get that you are trying to be funny, but yes. I do want to write a note on a napkin for him." I snagged a pen off the counter beside the register and drew a large heart on a napkin. Inside the heart, I wrote *I really enjoyed last night*.

She shook her head. "When did you get to be so sappy?"

"I'm happy, not sappy. Maybe we need to find you someone. Then you can be happy like me."

Tessa's eyebrows pinched together. "First of all, I *am* happy. Second, unlike you, my future plans do not include anyone else. It'll be me and my doughnut shop for years to come."

"I'm not going to argue with you, but I will say I told you so when some guy sweeps you off your feet." I stuffed the note into the bag with an extra napkin. Then prepped Eli's coffee.

"Did you get that lid on correctly?" Tessa was in kind of a mood. Maybe she didn't like my comment about being swept off her feet.

I let her check the lid. "What kind of doughnut does he get?"

"Plain glazed."

Who would have guessed?

I switched the sign to open and smiled as Eli walked in.

"Well, good morning." He flipped the sign to closed and grinned as he pulled me close.

"Hello, I'm right here." Tessa waved her arms.

He waved at her but stayed focused on me. "This is a nice surprise."

This time kissing in the doughnut shop didn't end with coffee spilled on my shoes.

"I have to run. I'll call you later." He kissed my cheek after picking up the bag and his coffee. "Thanks, Tessa."

"Bye." She walked out of the kitchen.

I followed Eli outside. "Have a good day."

"Thanks. We'll have to see how many tearful women weave and speed through the county today." He tipped his hat.

I stayed on the sidewalk and watched as he drove away.

Tessa opened the door. "Want another doughnut?"

"Just more coffee. Definitely more coffee. I did not get enough sleep last night." I hopped onto my favorite stool.

"Tell me all about the date." She glanced at the clock. "That sign can stay flipped for another few minutes."

For the next five minutes, I told her all about horseback riding, chatting over dessert, and dancing. "It was, by far, the best first date I've ever had. Shoot. The best date. Period. And he didn't leave me wondering if I'd hear from him again."

"Yeah, I'd say that his behavior this morning made that pretty clear."

* * *

THAT NIGHT, fifteen minutes after the end of his shift, Eli called.

"Hello."

"Thanks for the note. Did you have a good day?" He sounded tired.

"Pretty good. I shopped for furniture, but I haven't

bought anything yet. Not until the house is ready. How about you?"

"It wasn't too bad. I was going to suggest dinner, but I'm beat. Maybe tomorrow night?"

"Sounds good." I could really get used to dating a good guy. "I won't keep you. Go home and sleep."

"Yes, ma'am. Will I see you in the morning?"

"Unless I oversleep." I'd have to set an alarm.

"I hope that doesn't happen. Sweet dreams."

I said what I knew he was thinking. "You'll be in them."

"I hope so."

I smiled at the phone after hanging up. Talking to Eli at the end of my day became my new routine.

* * *

AFTER SEEING Eli every morning for several days, on Thursday morning, I slept in. Eli wasn't working, and I didn't think he'd be up early to get doughnuts. And as late as we'd talked last night, I needed a little extra shut-eye.

Intending to sleep for only a few minutes, I panicked when I opened my eyes and saw the time. The shop opened in thirty minutes.

I yanked on jeans and a blouse. I had just enough time to run next door for coffee and something to eat. I didn't want to try to run the store on an empty stomach.

Eli's knock echoed in the hall, and I ran to the back door. "Hi!"

He held up a bag and a cup. "You never showed up, so I figured you needed breakfast delivered."

I hugged him.

He kept his arms out to his sides. "Um, Delaney, please don't make me spill anything on you today."

"Sorry. Come in. I overslept." I gathered my hair into a messy bun. For today, that would have to do.

He handed me the coffee. "Someone keep you up late?"

"Way too late."

Leaning against the wall, he crossed his arms. I loved how it stretched the sleeves on his T-shirt. "If you're free tonight, I'd like to take you to dinner."

"It's a date." I bit into the doughnut. "You got my favorite."

His smile made me want to close the shop and spend all day with him, but that was no way to run a business.

"I pay attention."

"Are you going to work on the car today?"

"I have other stuff I need to get done today." He blew me a kiss. "Have a great day, and I'll be here when the shop closes."

"See you then."

It was too soon to be thinking of words like love and future. And way too soon to be naming our children, but dang. Eli made me want to think all those things.

Clearly, I still needed a dose of patience.

CHAPTER 17

I changed three times before settling on a summery dress and a pair of wedges. Eli hadn't said where we were going to dinner, but I wanted to be prepared for anything.

After freshening my makeup, I dabbed perfume on my pulse points. The butterflies migrating across my midsection weren't caused by nerves, just excitement and anticipation.

When Eli knocked, I hurried to the door. "I'm ready."

"Hi." He closed his eyes and inhaled. "Have I mentioned that I love that perfume? I think I love it because whenever I get a whiff, I think of you."

There were so many things that made me think of Eli. I wasn't sure I wanted to tell him that I thought about him every time I stepped into the shower. Or locked the door. Or picked up my phone.

It was way too early in the relationship to sound clingy and desperate.

I tugged him inside. "Let me grab my keys."

"You look beautiful." It was like Eli was trying to make me blush.

After stuffing my keys and phone into my purse, I clasped his hand. "Thanks. I wasn't sure where we were going. I hope this is okay."

He kissed my hand. "Hand me the keys, and I'll lock up. Did you set the alarm?"

I checked the alarm panel and dropped the keys into his hand. "Now it is."

Once the store was secure, we strolled to his truck.

"You aren't going to tell me where we're going, are you?"

That dazzling grin lit up his face. "You like surprises."

Eli went out of his way to surprise me. While I loved the attention, what I loved most was that he listened and tailored his surprises, knowing exactly what would make me smile. He treated me better than some of my own family.

He pulled into the winery.

"How did you get a reservation?" I'd called the restaurant about getting a reservation to surprise him and had no luck.

"I know Joji. When I mentioned to her that I was hoping to take you to dinner here, she called Jeffrey. We'll be at his table. And you said that was a good table."

"Joji is amazing."

Eli nodded. "Clint would agree with you. She's pretty great."

"Having dinner here is a nice surprise. Thank you."

He squeezed my hand before speaking to the hostess, and she ushered us to Jeffrey's table. Felipe was the waiter again.

He smiled as he walked up to the table. "Evening, so nice to see you again." He tipped his head toward Eli. "Is it still too soon to tell?"

"Definitely someone special." I patted Eli's hand, knowing he was probably confused by the cryptic conversation.

"Wonderful." Felipe smiled. "The chef will be out to speak with you soon. What can I get you both to drink?"

We told him what we wanted, and he hurried away.

Eli raised an eyebrow. "You going to explain that little exchange?"

"The last time I was here, Felipe was my waiter. I was texting you here at this table, and he asked if it was someone special. I'd said it was too soon to know."

"But now you know."

"You are definitely special."

I couldn't read the look on his face, but I didn't have much time to study his expression before Jeffrey walked up.

The chef made casual conversation, then told us the daily specials. As soon as Jeffrey left, Felipe was back and ready to answer questions.

Once Eli and I were alone and waiting for our food, he pulled in a deep breath. "I've tried to keep my mouth shut about you living in the strip mall, but it bugs me."

"It's only a few more weeks." Weeks sounded shorter than months, and I hoped that would end the conversation.

"What if I found you a place to live for those few weeks?"

I pulled my hand away from his. "I don't need you finding me a place to live."

He rubbed his jaw. "I don't like you living there."

"It's not your choice, Eli. I'm an adult. I can decide where I want to live." I folded my arms, angry that this perfectly romantic evening was being soured by this disagreement.

His boot bumped my foot. "I know it's your choice. And I'm not trying to dictate what you should do. But if money is the reason, I'd be willing to help with that."

"No. I can't let you do that. There hasn't been a hint of trouble at the store."

He leveled a gaze at me. "When I responded to that alarm, you were in a towel. What if that had been an intruder?"

"I seriously doubt bad guys would want to break in to steal lingerie."

"Burglars aren't expecting people to be in those stores

after hours. And when they get surprised, the results are sometimes tragic." He clenched his jaw. "But I'll drop it."

"Thank you. I'll think about what you said."

He nodded, but it was obvious he wasn't happy with that. "Tell me about the house."

"They've made a lot of progress. Soon, if you have time, I'll give you the grand tour."

He laid an open hand on the table, and I rested my hand on his.

"I'd like that."

* * *

BY THE END OF DINNER, I'd almost forgotten about our little spat. Almost. Eli could be opinionated, and maybe I didn't agree with him all the time, but I still liked him.

We strolled to his truck hand in hand.

He opened my door like he always did, but instead of helping me in, he pulled me close. "I have a surprise for you. There is someone I want you to meet."

I couldn't even guess who he wanted me to meet. "Okay." I glanced around.

"Not here. Hop in."

I buckled into my seat. "You know how to build anticipation."

He drove down the block and turned into Tessa's complex.

"Are we going to Tessa's?"

"Yep." He ran around and opened my door. "She played sitter for me."

Blood pooled in my toes, and I stopped. A sitter? Eli had a kid? And Tessa hadn't told me? Eli hadn't told me! I softened my shocked expression, trying to figure out what to say.

Eli let loose a deep belly laugh, and I snapped out of my tangle of thoughts.

"What's funny?" I'd clearly missed something.

He worked to catch his breath. When he did, he squeezed my hand. "I didn't think about how it sounded until I saw your face. Sorry about that. I do *not* have a child. I'm not keeping those kinds of secrets." After tugging me into a hug, he kissed the top of my head. "Didn't mean to shock you."

"It wouldn't be a deal breaker." There was so much about my past I hadn't told Eli, and because of my past, I would've embraced the child without question. "Kids are great. I was just surprised. And I wondered why it hadn't come up."

He leaned down to look me in the eye. "There are no children, no greedy ex-wives, and no bitter ex-girlfriends. There are a couple of ex-girlfriends, but as far as I know, they aren't bitter. They broke up with me."

"How did you manage to get a girlfriend?" It was easier to hide the effects of the shock by teasing him.

"Ouch, Delaney. That hurts." The twinkle in his eye said otherwise.

"Because you get so quiet. You know what I mean."

"Dating someone you aren't attracted to is a surefire way to end up with an ex-girlfriend." The look in his eye left no doubt of his attraction now.

"When you first mentioned the surprise, you said you wanted me to meet *someone*. So when you said sitter, I naturally thought…"

"*Someone* was a poor word choice, but if I say any more, it'll ruin the surprise." He pointed to the walkway. "And I really want to see the look on your face. Now more than ever." He lifted an eyebrow.

"Well, go on then. Surprise me." I inched up and planted a kiss on his chin.

Those green eyes sparkled as he cupped my face and

leaned in closer. His arm tightened around me as his lips touched mine. I slid my hands up his chest and looped them around his neck. Then I pulled myself closer to him.

As his lips moved against mine, he lifted me off my feet and walked, presumably to Tessa's door. I'd never been carried while being kissed before, but I'd highly recommend it. How could Eli even see his way to the door?

He broke the kiss, then pressed another one to my forehead.

"Wow."

"And that wasn't even the surprise." He knocked twice before turning the knob.

"Thank goodness you're here." Tessa sighed as a puppy— the one I'd so desperately wanted—ran circles around her feet.

I dropped to my knees and let the puppy lick my face. "He's yours?"

Eli squatted beside me. "I picked him up this afternoon, and I was hoping you'd help me choose a name for him."

Holding the wiggly puppy, I laughed. "What about Cumberbatch?"

"I am *not* naming my dog Cumberbatch." Eli shook his head to emphasize his point.

"Sherlock?" I snuggled the cutest puppy in the world.

Eli nodded. "I like that."

"I'm just going to let y'all cuddle together. Call me if you need something." Tessa pointed down the hall. "I'll be in my room."

"Did you know that I wanted this puppy? Before I went to Joji's, I went to the pet store that was hosting the adoption. I was so bummed when I found out some guy had already adopted him."

"I knew you wanted *a* puppy, but not this particular puppy. Tessa said you weren't going to get one until your house was finished." He scratched Sherlock on the tummy. "I didn't mean to steal him away."

"I feel better now that I know he has a good home and will be loved."

Eli nodded. "Probably spoiled a bit."

"And I can visit him."

"I hope you do."

I leaned close to Eli and dropped my voice to a whisper. "Oh, and by the way, the lady at the pet adoption thought you were hot."

His eyes widened. "What?"

"Smart woman." I went back to nuzzling Sherlock. "Wasn't she? You are pretty cute yourself. But he kisses better. No offense."

Sherlock whipped his tail back and forth, and Eli laughed.

Who knew that all of this was what hid underneath Eli's quiet exterior?

"What do you say we take Sherlock to my place so that Tessa can have her apartment back?" Eli looked down the hall. "If you haven't figured it out, she's not really a dog person."

With Sherlock in my arms, I stood. "Bye, Tessa."

She walked out and pointed at me. "I'll see you first thing in the morning."

"I'll be there."

Eli shook his head. "Are y'all planning to talk about me?"

I bumped his side. "What do you think?"

* * *

FRIDAY MORNING, I overslept and didn't have time to talk to Tessa, but I made up for it on Saturday morning by arriving at the doughnut shop before it opened.

"Morning, Tessa."

"Good morning. Big plans today?" She tied on her apron.

"Eli is working, so I'm pet sitting."

"Better you than me. That little guy is cute but not conducive to relaxation." She laughed.

"When did you talk to Eli about me wanting a puppy? I thought y'all didn't talk about me." I wiped down the coffee station.

She loaded doughnuts into the display case. "He already knew you wanted a puppy. I didn't tell him that. On the Friday you went to the adoption event, he messaged that morning asking when you were going to get one."

My phone buzzed, and I yanked it out of my pocket and read the message from Eli.

Sherlock and I are headed your way. Will you let Tessa know?

"Eli is headed this way." I grabbed a to-go cup and filled it with coffee. After prepping it to his specifications, I made sure the lid was on properly.

"He's texting you now?" Tessa laughed. "Tell him not to bring that dog into my shop."

I tapped out a text, warning Eli. *I'll meet you out front and put Sherlock in my store.*

He knocked on her door a few minutes later, and I ran out.

"Good morning." I hurriedly unlocked the door of my store.

Eli followed me in and set the crate down. "Tessa doesn't want dogs in her doughnut shop or were you just trying to get me alone?"

"Yes, and even though the second part hadn't occurred to me, yes." I stepped closer and slid my hands up his chest. "You're kinda hot in that uniform."

"Even with the body armor?" Chuckling, he lifted me off my feet and kissed me, making my morning even better. "Thanks for watching Sherlock today. He's just too little for me to leave for long, and I can't exactly tote him around with me."

"That would be funny. And you know I don't mind a bit. How did last night go?"

Eli scrubbed his face. "I'm tired. He woke up several times. I think his bladder holds about as much as a baby spoon. It can't be bigger than a peanut."

"Aww. I'm sorry. It's really okay if we go to your place?" I squatted in front of the carrier, greeting Sherlock.

"It's fine. I'm thinking a dog in a lingerie shop is a bad idea." He motioned to the racks behind him but didn't turn around. "The trailer isn't locked. Joji knows you'll be there."

"Great. Anything I need to know?"

"The llamas usually make a humming noise before they spit at you, and they don't seem to like it when I hum back. So, I recommend not doing that. And stay out of the goat pens. Boingo jumps fences, but he's mostly harmless. If there is another goat with him, don't bend over. Bumpo has earned his name." Eli scratched his head. "That's all I can think of."

I squatted in front of the carrier. "Sherlock, I'll be right back, buddy."

The puppy looked genuinely sad that we were leaving.

"I made sure to put the lid on your coffee properly." I clasped Eli's hand after locking the door.

"Much appreciated."

As soon as Eli left, I finished the last of my coffee and tossed my napkin in the trash. "Bye, Tessa."

She waved. "Call me later."

I stopped in the shop only long enough to grab my purse, a book, and Sherlock. Then I loaded it all in my car and drove to Eli's.

It would be a little weird being at his house while he wasn't there. Snooping was not part of my plan. But maybe a few peeks here and there would be okay.

"Hey, Sherlock, what do you want to do today?"

He barked an answer I didn't understand.

"I guess we'll just have to play it by ear."

I parked in front of the trailer just like I used to do when I visited Cami. As I unloaded the dog crate, a goat bounded toward me.

"Hello, you must be Boingo."

Boingo made a goat sound, and Sherlock barked.

"Have y'all met?" I set the crate down, letting Boingo and Sherlock sniff each other.

Boingo didn't seem that impressed. After a sniff, he trotted away, probably looking for some other trouble to get into.

I carried the crate inside and opened its door. Sherlock was more than happy to be released from his confinement and ran around the living room in circles.

On the counter was a note.

Delaney-

I left a little something for you in the fridge. I wasn't sure what your favorite flavor was.

And I might use fingerprint powder on the knobs to know where you snooped. (Joking... sort of.)

Call if you need anything.

E

I needed to wipe all the knobs even for the rooms I didn't enter. I opened the fridge and startled Sherlock with my laugh. Sitting front and center on the shelf were cans of Shasta soda in several different flavors.

Eli knew my first name.

How long had he had that tidbit? Until today, he hadn't made a single joke. And this teasing was cute. My thoughts jumped to the day he'd pulled me over. Eli had known my real name for a while.

There were lots of layers under that quiet shell. Should I be worried that he could keep a secret that well?

I dropped onto the floor and loved on Sherlock. We had lots of time to play.

* * *

AFTER HOURS of playing inside and out, Sherlock finally took a nap. I went through the fridge to see what food there was. Tonight, I'd surprise Eli with dinner.

In between play times with Sherlock, I spent the afternoon cobbling together a meal I hoped Eli would like.

A few minutes after seven, he texted: *You still at my place? Want me to pick up dinner?*

Still at your place. I have dinner covered.

He sent a thumbs-up, and I waited.

When Eli walked in the door after his twelve-hour shift, he sniffed. "Something smells good, and I don't just mean your perfume."

"I made dinner."

He petted Sherlock and grinned. "This is a nice surprise. Let me change really quick."

"Don't bother dusting the knobs. I wiped them all down to clear away any prints."

He laughed.

As I watched him walk down the hall, I thought of what he'd said when we were under the big oak tree. "There are always butterflies." It was true. My heart fluttered anytime he was near, and I never wanted that feeling to fade.

CHAPTER 18

*A*few days later, I parked near the end of my driveway, leaving enough room for Eli to turn in and park. I was finally going to give him a tour of my house. It was still hard to picture the place finished, but with the framing up, it seemed more like a house.

Eli's truck pulled in a minute later, and he grinned as he stepped out of the truck. "One thing I like about this place—it's very close to where I live."

"I was driving out to Cami's—which is now your place—when the realtor was putting the sign up. I pulled over and wrote down the number, but I also chatted with her that afternoon. I put in an offer right away." I tilted my head up to meet his kiss. "It's a dream come true."

"How many acres? It looks like it goes back a ways." He followed behind as I pulled him toward the house.

"Three acres. The house is set back off the road, but there is plenty of room to fence in space behind the house." Usually, I mentioned having a dog when talking about the fence, but tonight, I left that part off. We were very early in the relationship, but if things worked out with Eli, I wouldn't be getting a puppy because he already had the perfect puppy.

He stepped onto the slab. "Sherlock will love that."

"This is the front porch. It curves around to that side of the house. Eventually, I'd love a porch swing out here. Maybe a few rocking chairs."

"That would look great." He walked around the side, then back.

I pretended to open the front door. "And this is the house. The living room and kitchen are open. There will be an island there with barstools. The eating area is over here. There will be windows all around here, and I made sure there was room for a big table. Something big enough for family gatherings." That probably sounded silly since I'd said little about my family. But I'd decided that I needed to create my own family. This house was a huge part of working toward that dream.

"A long farmhouse table with chairs all the way around or will you go with a bench on one side?"

"I love the idea of a bench. I'll have to see what I can find. But until the place is done, I'm not buying anything. I'd only have to pay to store it." I led Eli into the room next to the kitchen. "This is the pantry and laundry room. The doorway over there leads to the garage."

He walked through into the garage. "Nice and deep. It looks like they are putting the water heater out here. That's good."

We continued through the house, and I showed him the bedrooms. "This will be my craft room. I'm having him add cabinets to this wall."

"That'll be awesome storage."

I felt a little like a kindergartener showing off artwork. "What do you think?"

"This is impressive, Delaney. Seriously. It's laid out well.

Spacious. This will be a great house." He strolled to where the back door would be. "Do you know who owns the land on the other side of the fence?"

"It's a working ranch. Star something. I'm trying to remember the name the realtor told me."

Eli glanced back over his shoulder. "Stargazer Springs? That's Beau Henry's place."

"That's it. I think you do know everyone in this town." I slipped my hand in his. "What do you know about the ranch?"

"Clint is the foreman."

"Joji's Clint? So, he's Lilith's Beau? I hadn't put that together. They've always been super nice anytime I've seen them."

"They're good people." Eli pulled me closer. "The next time there is a meteor shower, we can throw a blanket down in the grass and watch the stars."

"I'd love that." I loved that he was talking about our relationship like it would last. I wanted it to last.

* * *

CAMI STROLLED into the store right after lunch on a Friday. "Hey, there!"

"Hi!" I hadn't seen Cami since Eli and I had moved from talking on the phone to actually dating, and it wouldn't at all surprise me if she brought up Eli. "How's the social media business?"

"Busy. But I just got paid, so I came in here to find something nice."

I hurried over to a rack. "In my last shipment, there were so many cute pieces. These rompers." I held up one for her to see. "Check out this baby doll."

Her face lit up. "I love that one! Why do you have to make

135

it difficult? I came in here for that corset I've been eyeing." She took the baby doll. "But Harper would adore this."

"Of course he would. It's adorable, and it will look fabulous on you." Knowing Harper had already purchased the corset, I did my best to steer Cami in a new direction without her being any the wiser.

She strolled over to the corset and picked up the hanger. "How are things with you and Eli?" Her gaze danced between the baby doll and the corset.

"Really well. We've gone out a few times."

"Yay!" She put the corset back on the rack. "I just knew it would work. It was the night you went to Joji's, wasn't it?"

"You and Joji were in cahoots, huh?"

"You better believe it. I knew if I could get Eli to talk to you that he'd figure out that he liked you. Well, he already liked you. He just needed a little shove." She laid the lingerie on the counter and crossed her arms. "If y'all end up together, that'll be one more matchmaking success for me."

"For you?"

Her nose crinkled. "I get to claim at least partial success. Please. I played a hand in it."

"I'm not sure Eli needed anyone's help. He'd been stopping by and texting me even before I went to Joji's." What I didn't tell Cami was that the night on the goat farm had been a key turning point. "But thank you for arranging that evening. It was a nice surprise."

She rubbed her hands together. "Now that y'all are on your way to a happily ever after, I need a new project."

"It's kind of soon to—"

Her hand shot up. "Y'all are totally meant for each other. I can tell. And I know who needs a fella."

"Who?"

"That author lady. I think her name is Tandy."

I slapped a hand over my mouth. "For real?"

Cami waggled a finger at me. "Love isn't just for the young. Surely, there is an older gentleman here in the area who will tickle her fancy."

"I'd recommend not using the words man and tickle in the same sentence around Tandy. It'll spark a conversation you don't want to hear."

Laughing, Cami dug through her purse. "She asks all the men around here to pose without a shirt. Joji told me about the time when Tandy asked Clint. He just walked off. Has she asked Eli?"

"Not that I know of."

She slapped her credit card onto the counter. "Well, I've seen Eli without a shirt, and he'd definitely look good on a cover. Don't take that the wrong way. You know I'm not interested in Eli."

"I know." I stuffed the receipt in the bag with her purchase. "It was good talking to you."

"We need to get together. Maybe a double date."

"That'd be fun."

"I'll have Harper set it up with Eli." She waved as she strolled out of the shop.

I picked up my phone and smiled at the message from Eli. *There is a meteor shower tonight.*

I knew how I'd be spending my evening.

CHAPTER 19

*A*lmost two months later, I sat on the garage floor, keeping Sherlock entertained, while Eli rebuilt the carburetor.

Boingo sat next to him, occasionally jumping up to see what was happening on the workbench. Eli and I had seen or talked to each other every day, and there was no doubt we were a couple. Fears that his attraction would fade had waned. No longer was I executing a plan to create a happily ever after. I was just enjoying life.

I held fast to the end of a rope toy while Sherlock wrestled the other end of it. "Eli, why'd you get a dog?"

He glanced back over his shoulder. "Is this a trick question?"

"I'm curious. You never mentioned that you wanted a dog." I pulled Sherlock into my lap when he flopped down. "I think I've worn him out."

"Maybe he'll sleep a little longer tonight." Eli shooed Boingo away from the workbench, then wiped his hands before strolling over to where I was sitting. "I'd wanted a dog for a while. I hadn't planned on getting a puppy, but you told me you wanted a puppy. That's when I started looking for one because I figured it would give me something to talk to you about. I didn't say anything when we talked on the phone because I wanted you to be surprised when I finally found one." He scrunched up his nose. "And that makes me sound really silly."

"I think it's sweet. When did I tell you I wanted a puppy?"

"When I pulled you over."

"Oh. I've sort of blocked the memory of that whole night."

"I haven't." Those green eyes sparkled.

I stood and wiped dirt off the seat of my pants. "Whatever. You stared at the wall the whole time. You probably don't even know what color my towel—"

"Purple."

My cheeks burned, and the gleam in his eye left no doubt that my face was as red as the flashing lights on his cruiser. I scanned the room, hoping for a new topic of conversation.

I nodded toward the table where his carburetor was still in pieces. "How much longer?"

"I'm done for tonight. Let me get cleaned up, then I'll take you to dinner."

"What if we pick something up and eat here?"

He picked up Sherlock. "I like that even better, and I bet Sherlock loves that idea. Don't you, boy?"

"I can't wait until the house is finished. Then I'll be able to keep him at night when you work. Contractor said three more weeks."

"My parents don't seem to mind having him stay over. I think my mom is worried that it's the closest she'll get to a grandbaby. And speaking of my parents…" He pursed his lips as if he were trying to decide what to say.

I braced myself. If he suggested I live with his parents for three weeks, I might say something I'd end up regretting.

Then logic kicked in, and I trailed my hand down his arm, then laced my fingers with his. "I'd love to meet them."

"Good. I was thinking something casual. Burgers by the pool or something like that." He set Sherlock on the porch and opened the door. "I'd really like for you to meet them."

"Sounds like fun."

The wonderful grin spread across his face. "I'll set it up."

* * *

Five days later, I sucked in a deep breath as Eli ran around to open my door. His parents' single-story ranch-style home was surrounded by oak trees. Instead of pristine grass, wildflowers grew on each side of the front walk.

"You grew up here?"

He held out his hand. "I did. And if you're nice to me, I'll let you see my old room."

The next house was halfway down the block. "You had lots of space to roam."

"Yeah, Tessa and I found our fair share of trouble growing up. The stuff that got us into trouble was mostly my idea, so I felt bad about that."

I knew they'd been close growing up, but I was getting a better sense of how close. "She's like a sister to you, isn't she?"

"She is. Her mom worked, so she stayed here a lot. She liked being here more than being at home, I think."

The conversation only mildly helped to distract me from my nervousness. There was no reason to be nervous. Eli's parents were nice people. Tessa spoke highly of them. None of that mattered to my stomach. The butterflies in there were having a rave.

"You really have nothing to worry about." Eli rubbed circles on the side of my hand.

"I didn't say anything about being worried."

He shook his head. "Darling, I can read you like a book."

I was beginning to both love and hate that about him.

He lifted Sherlock out of the back seat and grasped the leash before setting him on the ground. "You brought your suit, right?"

"All right. I'm nervous." I couldn't help but wonder if I'd ever seen his parents around town but didn't know who they were. "What if they don't like me?"

"I don't care if they like you." He sounded almost convincing.

I stopped walking and inched up to kiss him. "Nice try."

He dipped his head to meet my lips again, and the front door opened.

Sherlock took off running, nearly pulling Eli over sideways.

"You made it." A woman at least four inches shorter than me spread her arms wide. "I can't tell you how excited I am."

Sherlock barked and ran in circles near the front door, dragging the leash behind him. Thankfully, Eli had the presence of mind to let go. Sherlock was excited about being at Grandma's house. Someone spoiled their granddoggy, it seemed.

"It's so nice to meet you." I hugged her and was nearly smothered. Maybe I'd been worried for no reason.

"I'm Patsy, Eli's mom." She hugged me again. "I've been asking Eli when I'd get to meet you. He's been talking about you for weeks."

Eli cleared his throat. "Why don't we head out to the pool?"

He'd been talking about me.

I slid my hand into his, and he squeezed my fingers without looking at me.

"You are lovely. Just beautiful. Eli has said that a hundred times, and he's right." She waved me in. "David is on the patio. He has the burgers on. All the fixin's are ready. We even have tomatoes fresh from the garden. David picked them this morning."

Eli tugged me close as she walked inside. "I hope you still like me after today."

"So far, I like you more."

"Is it because I said you were beautiful or because of the homegrown tomatoes?" He glanced toward the back door. "Hang on." He ran outside. "Mom, don't give Sherlock a hamburger. I don't want him learning to beg."

"It's just a tiny piece. Watch this." She held up the meat, and Sherlock perched on his haunches.

I eased up beside Eli and rubbed his back. "That's some pretty impressive begging."

"He's such a smart dog." Eli's mom laughed. "Come on. Let's eat."

Eli pulled out a chair at the patio table. "She'll feed anyone who comes within a hundred feet of her."

"I like her."

"She's pretty great." He beamed.

I loved that Eli had grown up with lots of space to roam and parents who adored him. He'd turned out pretty great as a result.

Mr. Gallagher strode over and stuck out his hand. "David Gallagher. It's a pleasure to meet you, Delaney."

"Thank you. It's very nice to meet y'all."

He set a tray of burgers and toasted buns on the table, and Patsy set out platters and bowls with everything I could possibly want on a burger."

"There's lettuce, tomato, cheese, onion, grilled onions, mushrooms, bacon strips, guac, and pickles. Am I forgetting anything?" She clapped her hands together. "Condiments. Be right back."

Eli put a burger and bun on my plate. "Here, you'll never go hungry."

"When do I get to see your room?"

He shot me a side glance. "Later."

"And yes, I have my swimsuit on under my sundress. You did say by the pool."

"Good."

We all built our burgers, and Sherlock curled up near Patsy's feet.

"Eli dear, I put your laundry on your bed. It's folded, and the shirts are ironed." She handed Sherlock a chew bone.

Later, I'd be teasing him about the fact that his mother did his laundry.

At the end of the meal, Eli stood and stretched. "I'm going to give Delaney a quick tour."

"Is there anything I can do to help clean up before we do?" I stacked my plate on top of Eli's.

"Oh, no. I've got it." Patsy gathered the plates. "And just so you know, Eli usually offers to help. He's a bit distracted today."

"As long as you don't pull out my baby book, I think I'll be okay." Eli looped a finger around mine.

His mom laughed. "It's on the coffee table."

I dashed toward the door, and Eli played along until we were inside. Then he scooped me up.

"Eli!"

He strode down the hall, turning sideways so that I didn't bang my head or feet against the wall. "They like you."

I slipped my arms around his neck. "They're sweet. And I like that you've mentioned me to them."

His cheeks turned an adorable shade of pink. "I'm close to my parents, and you're important to me. It came up a few times."

"Now what's this about your mom doing your laundry?"

He set me down in front of a door. "I am capable of doing my own, but she offered. So, I let her," He pushed open the door. "This is my old room."

The walls were mostly bare.

"No posters of swimsuit models?" I poked him in the ribs.

He shook his head. "I used to have a few car posters up. Set your bag in here, and I'll give you a quick tour. Then we can go out to the pool."

He gave me the grand tour of the house, then walked me back to the room. "See you in a sec."

"Hey."

"Yeah?" He rested his shoulder against the doorframe, looking as sexy as ever.

I inched up on my tiptoes and touched my lips to his. "I like you."

Smiling, he pulled me closer. "I've never kissed anyone in my bedroom before." The door closed behind him as he walked me backward. "But just a quick one."

He flopped onto the bed, pulling me down on top of him and sending half of his laundry falling to the floor.

The door opened, and I dropped my head to his chest. This was embarrassing.

"Hey, Dad. Need something?" Eli's tone was strained.

"Mom wanted to know if you wanted ice cream sundaes before or after swimming." Mr. Gallagher glanced at the clothes on the floor. "I'll let her know you're thinking about it." He walked out, and the door closed with a bang.

I pushed off Eli and found my footing. "I'll meet you out by the pool."

"Sorry about that."

I shrugged. It wasn't as if we'd been doing anything wrong. Eli was incredible when it came to respecting my boundaries. And he didn't even know all the reasons I had them.

"I'll go tell them we want ice cream in the hot tub after we swim."

"Can't say I've ever done that."

He blew me a kiss before walking out the door.

I slipped out of my sundress and shoes, then pulled my coverup on over my swimsuit. Maybe his dad wouldn't say anything about what he saw. What were the chances?

At the back door, I stopped and scanned the patio. Eli stood with his back to me, talking to his dad.

I needed to set up a call so that Eli could talk to my dad. If I waited until he came for a visit, he might never meet Eli.

Reaching for the door handle, I froze when Eli yanked off his shirt.

Dang.

Seconds ticked by as I watched him rub sunscreen onto his neck and arms.

"He'll probably need help getting it on his back. You should go out there." Patsy patted my arm.

"Sure. Yeah." I opened the back door and stepped out. "I can help with that."

Eli flashed that wonderful grin. "And I'll return the favor."

After spending time with Eli's parents, it was easy to see how Eli had turned out to be such an amazing guy.

For the first time, I could imagine spending my life with someone. With Eli. And my happily ever after didn't seem like a faraway dream. Now it was a possibility.

CHAPTER 20

*W*hen we arrived back at Eli's, he sat on the sofa and tugged me into his lap. "I hope you enjoyed yourself today."

"I did. Immensely. Your parents were very sweet and made me feel welcome. There were a few embarrassing moments, but I'll live."

"If you're worried that my dad will think we're... you know, I can say something. Not sure what, but something."

Imagining that conversation made me laugh.

He furrowed his brow. "What? I'm trying to be considerate."

"I know, and it's sweet. But you don't need to say anything." I ran my finger along his collar. "I was at the back door when you took your shirt off, and I'm pretty sure your mom picked up on the fact that I'd never seen you without a shirt before. I might've stared a minute or three too long."

He grinned, clearly flattered. "Now you see why I live on a goat farm instead of at home. I love my parents. I do, but I don't want to live with them."

"I really did have fun today."

"Good." He laughed when Sherlock climbed into my lap, wanting to be part of the cuddle. "I've been thinking about how you can't do the things you like to do."

"I like coming over here and spending time with you. And Sherlock." I gave him a quick peck.

"What if you had a space to make a wreath *before* the house was finished?" He shifted me out of his lap, and Sherlock had no choice but to move. Then Eli led me down the hall. "I looked at some website about craft rooms, and it made my head swim. I wasn't sure what setup worked best, and it's only temporary. We can move stuff around if you need it arranged differently." He opened the door to one of the extra rooms.

In the middle of the room was a table, and behind it, shelving units were against the wall. Lying on the table was a gift card to the nearest craft store.

"Eli!" I ran a hand along the top of the table.

"The trailer is always unlocked, but I'll give you a key. And if I'm sleeping, just be a little quiet." He eased up behind me and slipped his arms around my waist. "I can't wait to see how your wreath turns out."

I leaned back into him. "I have no idea what to say. This might be the sweetest thing anyone's ever done for me."

"I want you to be happy. And if that means having fake flowers and some glitter in my house, I'm okay with that."

"You're amazing, Eli."

He chuckled, and the sound rumbled in his chest. "I'm keeping my dark side hidden until later in the relationship."

"Thanks for the warning." I pulled away but kept a tight grip on his hand. "You're probably wondering why I haven't mentioned my parents."

"I figured you'd say something when you were ready." He ran his thumb along my knuckles.

Sherlock followed as I paced in the living room for a few seconds. Eli moved to the couch and sat, patient and quiet.

When I was ready to reveal my skeletons, I snuggled into his lap. It was a way to be close to him and not have to look him in the eye while telling my story. "I don't talk about this part of my life much. You know that I lived with my grandma, right?"

"You mentioned that when we talked about Christmas on the phone one night."

"I want you to know the rest." I leaned my head back on his shoulder. "My parents divorced when I was five, and my mom loaded me into the car and left my dad. I don't remember much from when they were married. I'm guessing it wasn't great. My mom had no concept of rules or structure or anything. She did whatever she wanted and justified it in her own mind. When she decided on something, no amount of logic could change her mind. But anyway, when I lived with my mom, we moved a lot. Sometimes we lived in an apartment, and she left me alone a lot. I learned to make myself food and take care of myself. Other times it was worse, and we lived in her car. I'd hide in the back seat of her car while she was in the bar or motel, doing whatever it was she was doing. Back then, I had no idea. But now, it isn't hard to figure out how she spent those hours."

Eli's muscles tightened, and he hugged me a little closer.

"When I was seven, I called my dad one night when my mom was passed out. I told him I was scared and asked him to come get me. He left that night and drove from Texas to Oregon. I kept my mom's phone hidden and sent him updates about where we were because Mom never stayed in one place long. I wasn't sure what she'd say when he showed up, but she didn't seem all that disappointed." I sucked in a deep breath. "That was when I told my dad to call me Delaney instead of Shasta. I never want to be like my mom."

Eli trailed his fingers through my hair. "Do you still have contact with your mom?"

"For a while she'd call from time to time, but I haven't heard from her in years. Part of me would like to see her again just so she could see how I turned out. In spite of her." I pushed out of his lap and walked into the kitchen. "Want anything to drink?"

"Sure. Grab me a cola."

I grabbed two Shastas and snuggled beside him. "What I didn't know until I got back to Texas was that my dad had just gotten married again. My stepmom wasn't happy to see me. Oh, she smiled, but even at seven, I could tell it was fake. That night, I heard them arguing. The next day, my dad drove me to San Antonio to my grandma's house. The only time I ever saw him cry was when he walked off the porch and left me. But living with Grandma turned out to be wonderful."

Eli draped an arm around me and drew circles on my shoulder.

"Because of her, I had an idyllic childhood in spite of my crazy family. But she died when I was fifteen, and I went to live with my dad. My stepmom wasn't that upset about it because they had a five-year-old and a three-year-old, and I was free babysitting. But I always felt like an extra. After graduating high school, I moved out, put myself through school, and then I used the money my grandma had left me and started my business."

"How did you end up in Stadtburg?"

"Tessa. Originally, I planned to open in San Antonio, but I spent a few days scoping out places outside the city because the rent was cheaper. After looking at the space where my store is now, I stopped in to get a doughnut. Tessa was warm and friendly in a way that reminded me of my grandma. Your mom has that same quality."

Eli kissed my temple. "I wish I could've met your grandma. She sounds amazing."

"She was. And she would've loved you." I took the can out of his hand and set our drinks on the table before nestling into his lap. "My initial interest in you was sparked by your rugged good looks and that dazzling smile. I had no idea that being in your arms would feel like this, like I belong here."

He hadn't even said that he loved me, and I was talking about belonging. But carving out space for me in his house meant the world to me.

His lips brushed my ear as he whispered, "You do, Delaney."

CHAPTER 21

I lifted my head off the pillow and felt around for my phone. Why was it buzzing in the middle of the night? Normally, I would've slept through it, but when Eli worked the night shift, I woke up at the slightest sound.

After rubbing sleep out of my eyes, I picked up the phone. *Stay inside with the doors locked until you hear my knock. Do NOT open the door for anyone else.* Eli's text made it impossible to go back to sleep.

I lay there in the dark for thirty minutes, maybe an hour. Time did funny things in the wee hours of morning. When I heard a thunk near the back door, I sat up and tiptoed into the hall.

The handle jiggled.

I shot off a text to Eli. *Are you at my back door?*

If Eli wasn't the person at the door, I wouldn't hear the end of this. Eli would lecture about the dangers of living in a retail space. Hopefully, he could cope for one more week. The house was so close to ready.

The screen lit up with Eli's name. I swiped and whispered, "Hello."

"Move to the front of the store. Do not open the door for anyone except me. Hear me?"

"Yes." I hurried to the front.

"I'm on my way." Eli stayed on the line.

Peeking around the edge of the blinds, I watched as Eli ran across the street. Blatantly jaywalking. Was jayrunning a thing?

When he darted onto the walkway in front of the store, I touched my hand to the glass. He acknowledged with a quick tap, then motioned for me to move back.

Huddled near a rack of negligees, I waited. But I couldn't help a quick look every few minutes. Two other deputies were parked in the lot. Eli's vehicle was still parked across the street.

One more week. That was what I kept telling myself.

I glanced at my phone every few minutes, expecting that an hour had passed. Time dragged out as I waited.

Men shouted somewhere outside, and I burrowed into the corner, forcing myself not to go check on Eli. If I stepped outside, he'd be furious. He was trained to deal with bad guys. I wasn't.

The voices quieted, and I held my breath as footsteps approached the front of the store.

Eli tapped out his knock on the front door. Thank goodness! I peeked out just to make sure it was my favorite deputy before turning the bolt.

He burst in and clutched me to his chest. For several minutes, he stayed quiet. When he pulled back, he cradled my face.

"Only a few more days. No more than a week." I said that as much to reassure me as to reassure him.

Eli shook his head. "I won't be able to sleep. Please, will you stay at my place overnight until the house is ready? Please. For me."

154

"I don't…" Only one room in his house had a bed. "There isn't…"

"I'll stay here."

"Eli, I run a business here. You can't sleep during the day or even walk to the shower without customers seeing. That won't work."

He lifted my chin. "Tonight is my last night shift for a month. The house will be ready before I have to work nights again. It's just a week. Please."

"You've said that a lot."

"Is it working? I can beg." He acted like he was going to drop to his knees.

I pulled him back up. "All right. I'll pack a bag in the morning. Sherlock will be happy with the new arrangement, I'm sure." I patted his chest, acting braver than I felt. "You probably need to get back to work."

"I do. Tomorrow I'll fill you in on what happened tonight." He turned toward the door. "You okay?"

I nodded. "Thanks for looking out for me." There was a chance I wouldn't sleep the rest of the night, but he didn't need to know that.

His gaze swept over me. "It's kind of funny to me that you own a lingerie store but sleep in a flannel nightgown. It's cute though." He didn't give me time to respond before slipping out the door.

It closed behind him, and I bolted the lock.

He waved as he walked toward the other officers.

I hadn't even teased him about crossing in the middle of the street.

* * *

EVERY TIME I closed my eyes, I saw the knob on the back door jiggling. It brought back the fear from the nights huddled in my mom's back seat, hoping I wouldn't be spotted.

Sleeping was a lost cause. Two hours after Eli left, I rolled out of bed and packed a bag.

It would be a little weird sleeping in Eli's bed, but after all the commotion, I wasn't sure I wanted to stay overnight at the store. The thought of someone breaking in while I slept made me cold.

After changing out of my flannel nightgown and into leggings and a baggy T-shirt, I knocked at the doughnut shop long before it opened.

Tessa shoved the door open. "What's wrong? Why are you awake?"

"Someone tried to break into the store last night. I never got back to sleep." I pulled my hair into a ponytail. "I'm going to go to Eli's, but I didn't want you to worry about me. Issa is covering the store today, so I can go sleep for a while."

She hugged me. "I'm so sorry. Eli mentioned something happened. He showed up right after I arrived to make sure nothing was out of place in the shop. He's probably freaking out about it."

"You think? Until the house is finished, I'm sleeping at his place." I waggled a finger in her face before she could utter a word. "And he is sleeping in my store."

Tessa laughed. "Eli staying in a lingerie store is kind of funny."

"All kinds of funny, but I'm too tired to laugh about it right now." I pulled my phone out of my pocket. "I should probably warn Eli that I'm going over there."

I waved as I walked to my car, then texted Eli. *Can't sleep. Going to your house.*

The phone rang as I started the car. "Hey. You got my message."

"I'm glad you're going over there. Lock yourself in if it makes you feel more comfortable. I have a key."

"Thanks."

"I'll see you in a few hours."

"If I'm asleep, wake me. Okay?"

"Sure thing. Gotta go." He ended the call.

I drove to the goat farm. Boingo didn't run out to greet me. He was probably with the other goats, sound asleep.

Once I was inside, I dropped my bag near the door and flopped on the sofa. The man had no throw pillows, so I wandered back to his room and stole a pillow off his bed.

I lay down and closed my eyes. The pillow smelled like Eli, and feeling protected, I relaxed.

* * *

I SHIVERED and pulled the blanket up over my shoulder. Blanket? I hadn't grabbed a blanket. Prying my eyes open, I lifted my head.

Eli smiled. "I was going to wake you up... in a few minutes."

"I don't even want to think of how bad I look. I think I was drooling." I pushed up to a sitting position and tapped the couch.

He moved next to me. "You can go back to sleep. I'm about to crawl in bed. There is a doughnut for you on the counter. And coffee, but I'm not sure if it's still hot. I told Mom I'd pick up Sherlock this afternoon. Don't forget that we are having dinner with my parents tonight."

"Your mom's birthday dinner." I leaned my head on his shoulder. "Tell me about last night."

He sucked in a deep breath and held it for a few heartbeats before blowing it out. "A man in Bexar County shot his ex-girlfriend. There was a manhunt, and his car was found broken down on the interstate. He made his way into town on foot and searched for a place to hide out." Eli stroked my hair as he talked. "I texted you when they sent out word that his car had been found near our exit."

"Did he have a gun when they found him?"

"He did, but he was arrested without anyone getting hurt. They found him in the empty space at the end of the strip mall."

"You haven't said 'I told you so.' I'm a little surprised."

He flashed a small smile. "That would just make you mad. Then the automatic sprinklers would come on, and I don't handle tears well."

"Never would've guessed." I snuggled closer. "You jaywalked for me."

"I'd break a lot of rules for you, Delaney."

I didn't want him to break rules for me. Especially since I had no plans to break any more of my rules for him.

Some rules were not made to be broken. Those rules kept me from turning out like my mom.

CHAPTER 22

J'd stopped at my nearly finished house after leaving Eli's this morning and gotten good news. The final details were going to be taken care of this weekend, and after a walkthrough on Tuesday, my house would be finished.

Excited barely described how I felt.

Maybe I'd see if I could snag a reservation at Jeffrey's and take Eli out for a celebratory dinner.

The store stayed busy all day—even busier than normal for a Friday—and I didn't get a chance to call.

That afternoon, Tandy wandered through the racks, humming to herself. I'd started to think she came in for book research and inspiration more than to actually shop. But I liked seeing her.

She stopped near a rack of bralettes. "Have any more trouble with creeps?"

"Occasionally. There was a man in here this morning who bought a corset and garter and thought he was being clever by saying that he was shopping for his mom." I rolled my eyes.

"It's never for their mom." Tandy laughed. "That must be code for 'I'm telling a fib.' Don't you think?"

"I guess. I can't imagine anyone would actually believe it." The door opened, and I gasped. "Eli! You never come here when my shop is open."

The man rarely walked in farther than the back hall even when I was closed.

He nodded toward the racks. "I came here to shop. Today, I'm a customer."

"What are you looking for? I'll have to see if I have it in your size." I gave him the once-over. While I carried a limited selection of items for men, I knew better than to think Eli was shopping for himself. That begged the question. Who was he shopping for?

He grinned. "Not for me, but I'll definitely need your help."

"What did you have in mind?" I kept my voice low because Tandy did not need to hear me flirting with Eli.

"A robe maybe?"

I laced my fingers with his and led him to a rack. "Something like this?"

He smiled at the terrycloth robes. "These are nice."

"They come in several different patterns. I'm partial to the wildflowers." I took a brightly colored robe off the hanger and slipped it on. "It's a nice length. Below the knee, but not so close to the floor that you trip. And it has pockets."

"Pockets in a robe are important." He leaned in closer. "Where else would you put your keys when you go take a shower?"

My cheeks felt like lava, and that was before he trailed a finger along my jawline.

"What size do you need?" I leaned into his hand on my cheek.

"I'll take that one."

Tandy walked over and flashed a wide grin, completely interrupting our moment. "Well, don't you look cute modeling that robe!"

Her words sent an icy chill racing down every nerve. Modeling the merchandise. I'd broken another rule. He hadn't even asked me to do it. My panic tasted sour. I'd have to think about this when Eli wasn't around.

Breaking rules wasn't right. I had rules for a reason.

Now Eli was here shopping, and that made him a customer, which meant I'd broken all three rules.

Eli's brow furrowed as he stared at me. He could probably read my inner turmoil.

Tandy patted him on the arm. "You tell your mama hello for me."

"Yes, ma'am. I will." He barely glanced in her direction.

"If you change your mind about posing without a shirt for one of my book covers, you call me."

"No, ma'am. I won't." He waved as she walked out.

"Is this all? Just the robe?" I focused on keeping my breaths steady and even.

It wasn't Eli's fault that he'd made me break the rules. He hadn't suggested I put on the robe. But thoughts of all the men who had asked in the past flooded my thoughts.

Avoiding his gaze, I walked to the counter. "I can ring you up over here."

He followed me to the register. "I'm picking up another item. It should be paid for already."

We received very few phone orders, and I hadn't taken a call from Eli, so Issa must've handled it on Saturday. I picked up the bag with his name on the little yellow slip attached. How had I not noticed his name on an order?

I opened the bag to check for the receipt. "Would you like to see the…"

Inside the bag was a black lace negligee… in a medium.

I swallowed the lump in my throat and continued my question after too long a pause. "Um, the item. Would you like to look at it?" I forced myself to meet his gaze.

He looked at the counter. "No. I don't. I'm sure it's fine."

Was that guilt?

There were two possibilities, and neither made me happy. Either he'd bought it for me—I wore a medium—or he'd bought that black lacy thing for someone else. Both ideas made me mad, and I could feel hot tears burning my eyes.

"Do you need these wrapped?" I went through the motions, treating him like any other customer. Like a customer I wasn't dating.

When he didn't answer, I looked up.

He shook his head and laid a gift certificate on the counter. "Delaney, it's for my mom."

That was the final blow… or the last straw. Whatever. Eli had the nerve to come into my shop and lie to me about buying lingerie for another woman. How could he?

I shoved the receipt into the bag with the robe and handed him both bags. "Have a nice day."

"Delaney?" He leaned down, trying to catch my eye.

This was a horribly inconvenient time for him to be able to read me. "Is there anything else I can help you with?" I used my best customer service voice.

"Nope." He turned and walked out the door.

I waited until he was in the truck, then turned the sign around and locked the door. I didn't even bother to put up a note about why I'd closed early.

Tears were sliding down my face before I made it back to my room. I threw myself on the bed. For his mom. Did he think I was an idiot?

My phone buzzed and I picked it up, even though I knew it was probably Eli.

Not sure what I said that made you mad, but message me when you're ready to discuss it.

Eventually I'd have to talk to him. Some of my stuff was at his house. And Sherlock.

This was awful. My happily ever after disintegrated, leaving me with nothing but heartache and ashes.

I cried for a while, and then I must've fallen asleep. The next thing I remember was Eli's knock at the back door. I ignored it for two minutes, but it became abundantly clear that he wasn't going to stop.

"What?" I yanked the door open.

Tessa glared at me. "I should ask you the same thing."

I leaned out the door, wondering where Eli was. Not that I wanted to see him, but I'd heard the knock.

"He's not here, Delaney. He's not coming."

"But the knock?" I sounded as dull as I felt.

She rolled her eyes. "The knock code for E. You'd mentioned he used a super-secret knock. So, I asked him what it was."

"Some secret."

"He warned me that you might not answer if you thought it was him." She propped her hands on her hips and inhaled, looking more than ready to lecture me. "But you did answer, and that makes me think—"

I put my hand up. "I don't want to talk about it. Eli isn't who I thought he was, and I have to work through that."

Tessa wiped at tears. "I'm your best friend, right?"

"You know you are, and I hope breaking up with Eli won't change that."

She stepped closer and stuck her finger in my face. "You're wrong."

"He bought a black lace negligee and then had the audacity to tell me it was for his mom. It was a medium! She doesn't wear a medium. I've met her." I pulled my hair into a ponytail but let it fall without putting a hair tie on it. "And I modeled a robe for him."

"You are letting those stupid rules blind you." She spun around and stormed out.

Now I didn't have a boyfriend or a puppy. And I wasn't even sure I had a best friend.

I no longer felt like I belonged. Having a finished house didn't seem quite as exciting without anyone to celebrate with.

Home was about more than a structure.

CHAPTER 23

Saturday morning, I woke up with red puffy eyes and a text from Eli.

Please talk to me. I spent all night trying to figure this out, and I'm clueless. Not even Sherlock has a clue. And believe me, I asked. Multiple times.

My heart melted a little, but then I remembered what he'd said. I was nowhere near ready to talk to him. His whole awkward and bewildered act was almost believable. But Tandy's emphatic statement affirmed what I knew. It was never for the mom.

My gut said Eli was telling the truth, which meant that I needed to eat because my gut couldn't be trusted.

On Sunday morning, I woke up to another text, but it wasn't from Eli.

It was the first I'd heard from Tessa since Friday. I hadn't gone into the doughnut shop, so I couldn't just blame her for that.

I'll always be your friend. And Eli deserves to know why.

I tapped out a reply. *Thank you for being my friend.*

You're still wrong.

I wished with all my heart that Tessa was right, but I couldn't figure out any way she could be. She was at least right about one thing. I needed to be an adult and talk to Eli.

By Sunday afternoon, I'd mustered enough courage—or maybe it was just bravado—to unload on Eli. He wanted to know why I was mad, and I'd tell him. I hated that there would be tears, but that couldn't be helped.

I pounded on his door.

It opened only a little, and Sherlock ran out. Eli wasn't fighting fair. I dropped onto the top step and snuggled my puppy. Correction. Eli's puppy. Sherlock had grown so much since that very first night when I'd seen him at Tessa's. I hated that I wouldn't see him every day.

The door creaked, and Eli stepped aside. "Would you like to come in?"

"No." I stood and crossed my arms. "You can give my stuff to Tessa whenever. I'll get it from her."

"What happened, Delaney? What caused the wash of panic when Tandy commented on you modeling the robe? What caused the fury that had tears brimming in your eyes? Please tell me so that I can fix this." The crease in his brow made him almost convincing.

If I looked into those green eyes another second, I'd give in, so I dropped my gaze to the step. "I know it wasn't for your mom. She doesn't wear a medium."

"Well, crap. Can she exchange the robe for the correct size?" Eli was determined to keep up the farce.

Rapidly blinking, I hoped I could spew a little fire before the floodgates gave way. "Sure. She can return the robe *and* the *black negligee*. And if that's what you got your mom, that's an entirely different issue that I'm not qualified to discuss." I stomped down the stairs, then stopped. "Did you forget that I was at your mom's birthday dinner? You need to find a better lie."

Sensing the discord, Sherlock ran back and forth between me and Eli.

"I gave her my gift on her actual birthday. Did you say *black negligee?*" He raked his fingers through his hair. "That must be what—"

"Save your explanation. I've heard too many explanations." I wanted to make it back to my car before I started crying.

"I don't want to fight." He followed me.

I kept my back to him. "I thought you were different than those other guys."

"I am, Delaney. But I think you know that." He opened my car door. "You just won't stop long enough to listen to logic."

His implication that I was behaving like my mom burned in my chest. He'd used my own vulnerability to hurt me. Tears streamed down my cheeks. Not only was I mad at Eli, but I was also mad at myself for being open and honest with him.

Struggling to catch my breath, I climbed into my car. I'd been so convinced that Eli was one of the good guys, but he was like all the others.

When I made it back to the store, I called Tessa. "Hey, I have a favor to ask."

"What do you need?" She didn't sound happy.

"I told Eli to give you my stuff from his place. No hurry." I flopped on the bed and stared at the ceiling. "This really hurts."

"The pain is self-inflicted. You wouldn't even listen to him."

"He told you that I went over there?" Having his cousin as my best friend made this whole thing more complicated.

Sherlock barked in the background.

"I heard the whole thing."

"You're at Eli's? I didn't see your car." I spun my keys

around my finger, watching the tiny canister of pepper spray swinging back and forth.

She gave a small huff. "My car isn't here. Listen, I—" She sighed. "I know I promised. I'm not telling her." That last part was clearly not directed at me.

"Tessa! Not tell me what?"

"What I promised I wouldn't. He'll tell you when you give him a chance and listen to him. In person. I never asked to be in the middle of this." Her voice wavered. "You were both so happy. Didn't you like being happy?"

"If staying single is good enough for you, I might try it too." I wiped my eyes. "Give Sherlock a kiss for me."

"I am *not* kissing a dog. Call me later if you need to talk."

"Bye." I threw my phone across the room.

When it landed in multiple pieces, I regretted my tantrum.

Now I needed a new phone.

* * *

Monday morning, I skipped coffee and doughnuts but managed to open the store on time. Business was slow, but I made sure my smile didn't fade. If I could make it through today, I'd get the keys to my house tomorrow, and little by little, the ache would wane.

It had to.

Right now, breathing was a chore. I think it had something to do with the war going on between my gut, brain, and heart. So many times during the day, I reached for the phone, wanting to text Eli and ask for that explanation. But my phone no longer worked.

Mondays were normally long. This Monday lasted a lifetime.

Just before closing, the door opened, and when Eli's mom

walked in, my heart landed near my feet. I wasn't at all prepared to face his mom.

She flashed a wide smile, acting like my relationship with her son hadn't gone up in flames. "Hi. How are you? I haven't seen Eli since Friday, and he keeps me updated."

"I'm okay." Was that a vague enough answer? "Can I help you with something?"

"I hope so. My husband and my son—God love them— aren't good with sizes. Is it possible to exchange what they gave me? I haven't tried them on or anything. I don't think I could've gotten that negligee on my thigh." A full laugh bubbled out of her. "I asked David why he'd gotten me a medium, and do you know what he said?"

I shook my head.

"When he called in the order, he told the woman I was average size. Average. Love *is* blind."

I grabbed the counter, trying to keep myself from slamming into the floor. "Oh. That's funny."

"I probably have you to thank for helping Eli pick out such a cute robe. I love it. I just need a bigger size."

"I helped a little." Clicking the end of a pen over and over, I tried to quell my panic. "What did Eli tell you on Friday?" There was a big possibility I'd regret asking the question.

Her brow wrinkled. "About what?"

"Me."

She walked around the counter and rubbed my arm. "He was quiet. I didn't ask. Arguments are part of every rela- tionship."

After tossing the pen on the counter, I grabbed her hand. "I love your son." I was a horrible person for telling his mom before telling him.

Wiping her eyes, she grinned. "That makes me so happy."

My head swam with all the apologies I owed Eli. "Let me get you the correct sizes."

"Extra-large for both please." She waited at the counter as I picked out the right sizes. "Is your house finished? Eli mentioned that it was close a few days ago."

"The final walkthrough is tomorrow. They were staining some cabinetry today and a few other final touches." I folded the items and put them in a bag. "Thank you for stopping by. I'm glad we got those sizes sorted out."

"Me too." She answered a call as she walked out the door. "Hi, David. I can model my birthday present tonight. I have the right size now." Her laughter echoed as she walked to her car.

As soon as she was in the parking lot, I flipped the sign and locked the door. I needed to get to Eli's. With my phone shattered, I couldn't even text him to let him know I was on my way.

I exceeded the speed limit in my hurry to get to the goat farm and was glad I didn't get a ticket. I needed to see Eli and beg him to forgive me. Tessa had been right. I'd let those rules blind me. Eli had been right. I'd been so convinced I was right I wouldn't even listen to him.

As I turned into the goat farm, I spotted his truck. He wasn't working. I hadn't even considered that he might be working. Showing up at the station with a tear-stained face and asking for Eli would spark gossip, but if he didn't answer here, that was my next stop.

I jumped out and pounded on his door. "Eli, please answer. I need to talk to you."

Sherlock barked inside.

Boingo ran up the steps and sat beside me.

"Do you know where Eli is?" I held out hope that Boingo would run off the steps and lead me to where Eli was hiding.

But Boingo only cocked his head. Talking to a goat wasn't helping.

Sherlock barked again. Maybe Eli was inside, deciding whether to answer the door.

"I was wrong." After a few more bangs, I pressed my ear to the door. Sherlock was the only one making a sound.

I rested my forehead against the door. "Eli, I see your truck, so I'm guessing you're in there. You have every right to hate me and never speak to me again, but I need you to know that I love you. I should've trusted you. And I'm sorry."

If that didn't get him to open the door, then nothing would.

CHAPTER 24

*A*s I pulled out of the gate, I thought through Eli's schedule. He was supposed to be working today. Maybe someone had driven him to work. I couldn't imagine why, but there was an easy way to find out. I'd walk myself into the station and ask at the front desk.

We could deal with the gossip after the fact, but right now I didn't have a choice. I needed to apologize to Eli.

The sound of sirens snapped me out of my thoughts. The plume of smoke ahead was probably the reason. Grass fires weren't uncommon during the summer. Hopefully, the fire wasn't too close to my property.

I approached the bend on high alert, ready to slow down for emergency vehicles. When I saw the firetrucks at the end of my driveway, in front of my house, I slammed on the brakes. I launched out of my car and ran across the road, staying back to give the firefighters room to work. But it was obvious that no amount of water would make the house okay.

Smoke billowed from the roof and poured out of the windows.

It was completely destroyed.

With my arms wrapped around myself, I tried to keep what was left of me from falling apart.

Firemen shouted at each other as they dragged hoses around and doused the fire. Harper was out there, and he knew I hadn't moved in. I scanned the area in front of the house. There were only firetrucks here, no other cars or trucks. That probably meant there were no workers on site. At least the firefighters didn't have to be concerned about saving anyone from the fire.

Coughing, I moved so that smoke wasn't blowing into my face, choking me and making my eyes burn.

I jumped when one side of the house collapsed. There went the perfect master bedroom and delightful craft room. I'd lost everything. There was plenty to be thankful for. My stuff wasn't in the house. Tessa still spoke to me. And I still had a growing business.

Staring at my house as it turned to ash made me regret even more how I'd treated Eli. As horrible as it was to watch the fire, losing him hurt more.

More of the house collapsed, and all I could do was stare.

Warmth spread across my back as someone stepped up behind me. I could feel Eli's quiet strength. He tapped out the secret knock on my hip, letting me know he was there. For me. With me. I leaned back against his strong frame.

"You didn't answer the door." I held out hope that maybe he could forgive me. Someday.

His whiskers brushed my cheek. "I wasn't home. But I heard you stopped by."

I tilted my head to look at him. "And?"

His arms wrapped around my waist. "I love you too."

Someone—probably Joji—had filled him in on what I'd said.

"I owe you an apology."

He pressed a kiss to my cheek. "We'll talk about it later."

We stood for a long time with his arms holding me up and neither of us speaking.

I hadn't lost everything. The most important thing in my life—no offense to Sherlock—was with me when I needed him most.

Eli loved me.

* * *

Firefighters were cleaning up their gear when Tessa and Cami walked up. Word had spread. The sun sank toward the horizon, and now that my heart wasn't pounding, exhaustion set in.

Cami wiped at tears. "I don't know what to say."

"There isn't really anything to say." I pulled Eli's arms around me a little tighter. "I have insurance. The builder has insurance. It'll get sorted out, and they'll build it again."

Tessa stood next to me. "I tried calling you. I'm so sorry."

"My phone broke when I threw it against the wall last night." I clasped her hand. "Thanks for being honest with me even when I was too stubborn to listen."

She glanced up at Eli. "He has many flaws, and I'll be happy to enlighten you about all of them, but cheating isn't one of them."

He rested his chin on the top of my head. "She's right. Except about the many flaws. A few maybe, but many feels excessive."

"Anything I can do?" Tessa squeezed my hand.

"Not really. There is nothing I can do right now anyway." I glanced back at my car. "I don't think I even turned off my engine."

"I did." Eli patted his pocket. "Your keys are here."

"Want to stay at my place?" She raised her eyebrows. "I'll

make you something good to eat."

"She's staying at my house." Eli snapped out the response, then looked down at me. "Aren't you?"

"Yeah, but thanks for the offer, Tessa. Eli and I need to talk about some stuff."

"That's an understatement." She winked. "Call if you need anything." Tessa walked over to where Cami was talking to Harper.

I turned and faced Eli. "You aren't mad at me?"

"Not anymore. I was, but I understand about your rules."

I'd never told Eli about my rules. "How did you know about my rules?"

"Let's grab dinner and talk at the house." He laced his fingers with mine.

I scanned the road for his vehicle. His Datsun was parked behind my car.

"You got it running!"

"Yep. I took some vacation time and finished up the last few things. I was headed to your store to offer you a ride and demand—and then beg—you to talk to me."

"I really thought you were lying to me."

"Just because no one shops for their mother in a lingerie store? You underestimate my awkwardness. I had a gift certificate that Cami and Harper gave me for Christmas. What else was I supposed to do with it? Shop for you? I knew better than to do that. And just for the record, I had no idea what was in the bag. I was picking it up for my dad. He said he was too busy to make it over there, but I think he wanted to avoid walking into the lingerie store. No offense to your store."

"I should've trusted you."

"Yep." He pulled my keys out of his pocket. "I have an idea. Tessa, Cami! Will y'all drive Delaney's car to the goat farm? I want to show off my car."

Tessa grinned. "Sure thing."

Eli helped me into the passenger seat. "We'll take the long way to go get dinner, and we won't talk about rules until later. Deal?"

"Deal." I kept hold of his arm. But the words I wanted to say didn't seem sufficient to convey how I felt.

He squatted beside the car, then gave me a quick kiss. "Dinner first then we'll talk."

"I love you. I'm not sure I could ever accurately describe how it felt to have you walk up behind me. I needed you, and you were there. Quiet and strong was exactly what I needed in that moment."

"I can guess how it felt. When you leaned back into me, I knew we'd be okay. I know how much that house means to you and wish I could rebuild it with a snap of my fingers, but having you is so much more important to me."

The disappointment made it clear what was most important. "I think the house must've already been on fire when I drove by on the way to your place. The firetrucks weren't here yet. I would've noticed that I think. Maybe not. But the house was too far gone when I got here for it to have started only minutes before. I wasn't at your place all that long." I rested my head against him. "I was in such a hurry to see you and to apologize that I didn't even look at my house. I just wanted to find you."

He cupped my cheek. "I'm here."

I kissed his palm. "Tell me about your car." Talking about the house would only spawn tears.

"Yes, ma'am."

Love wasn't a mushy feeling anymore. It wasn't butter-flies flapping around in my stomach, tingles dancing on my skin, or a happily ever after. Love was patient and kind, even when I hadn't been.

CHAPTER 25

*S*nuggled on the couch, I rested my head on Eli's shoulder.

"Sherlock is sure happy to see you." Eli stroked the dog. "He's been off-kilter the last few days."

"I'm so sorry." It was easier to stay focused on Sherlock and not look at Eli. "I cried myself to sleep Friday night. I was so mad. But you have to understand that I've had guys tell me that they were shopping for their mom. They act like it's funny or some inside joke. When you said that…" I looked up at Eli. "I don't know how to explain how it made me feel."

"Mad." He poked me in the side. "Guys have really said that? That's weird. If I'd had any clue what was in the bag, I would've done a lot more explaining then and there."

"But you didn't want to see what was in the bag."

"Does it surprise you at all that I didn't want to see what my dad bought my mom at the lingerie store? Really?"

The way he'd behaved that day made more sense without the cloud of anger and jealousy masking the truth.

"You asked about my panic when Tandy talked about the robe." I rubbed at the wrinkles in his T-shirt.

He trailed a finger along my jaw liked he'd done that day. "One minute we were flirting, and the next minute, you were looking at me like I was dangerous."

"Why did you get your mom a medium?"

"Delaney, when you were modeling that robe, I wasn't thinking about my mom." He grinned when I laughed.

Telling him about my rules would sound silly, and I asked another question, hoping to delay that part of the discussion.

"Tessa knew about you picking up the gift for your dad, didn't she?"

"Yep, but I made her promise not to say anything. She didn't need to be in the middle of it." He shifted me into his lap. "But I made her tell me about your rules."

"How is that fair?"

"We've already established that I have flaws. Do you want to hear my side or not?" He lifted his eyebrows.

"I'm listening."

"When I told her what happened, she mumbled something about rules. I hounded her until she spilled the beans." He wrapped his arms around me. "Then I understood. You and me, we like rules. And if I had you breaking your rules, I was a little bit dangerous." Soft lips pressed against my temple. "I know that not being like your mom is why you have rules. I'm sorry for implying you were acting like her."

"The truth hurts."

"I shouldn't have said it." He leaned his head on mine. "As soon as I did, the look on your face broke my heart. I worried you wouldn't forgive me even after you knew the truth."

"When I knocked and you didn't answer, I worried that you had reverted to the quiet Eli or that you'd lost interest."

He dropped a kiss below my ear, then continued down the side of my neck.

My rules had been so important to me that I'd given up good sense. "Rules have always been important. I never wanted to be like my mom, and she acted like rules didn't matter. But I put too much focus on my rules—which might've been the wrong rules to have anyway—and lost sight of what's most important."

Eli hugged me closer but didn't say anything.

"Will you forgive me?" I resisted the urge to bury my face in the curve of his neck. Instead, I held his gaze and waited for his response, knowing what he'd say and needing to hear it.

"Yes. I forgive you." He tapped out our secret knock on my hip. "And I love you, rules and all."

I tilted my head, giving him easier access. "When your mom came into the store to exchange things, I told her that I love you."

"I know. She called me."

"Did Joji tell you that I went to your house?" I tipped my head back as he kissed the front of my neck.

"Clint sent me a video."

"Video?"

"Doorbell cam. He thought it sounded important." Eli brushed his lips on mine. "He was right."

"You heard everything I said?"

He nodded. "Including what you said to Boingo."

"Why does your trailer have a doorbell cam? You don't even lock it."

"Because of the goats. Joji installed several on the property to catch the funny things they do." After kissing his way across my collarbone, he pulled back. "I should probably head over to the store. It's late, and you have to work tomorrow."

"What about you?"

"I'm not working." He stretched. "I'd already booked leave

so I could help you move in. I was going to surprise you. I'm off all week."

"I don't mind sleeping on the couch tonight, but we're going to have to figure something out because having you stay at the shop won't work when you are working nights. Women would die if they saw you in a towel headed to the shower. Shoot. I might die."

Eli laughed, full and loud. "I truly hope not."

Sherlock's head popped up, and he barked.

"Sorry, baby. We didn't mean to wake you." I patted Sherlock's head.

Eli yawned. "You go crawl in the bed. I'll sleep out here." He ran his fingers through my hair. "I'm glad we talked."

"Me too. And thank you for not telling your parents about how stupid I was acting."

"People who are in love argue. My parents don't need to know about every spat."

I straddled his lap and kissed him. "I love you, Eli Gallagher."

Gripping my hips, he made silent promises as his lips moved against mine.

From now on, I'd stick with one rule—trust my gut.

AT FOUR IN THE MORNING, I trudged out to the living room because Sherlock needed a potty break. After a whispered warning to be quiet, I opened the front door and stepped out onto the porch.

What I really wanted to do was take advantage of the fact that Eli was sleeping without a shirt and enjoy a few moments of gawking, but instead, I was watching a dog pee. Sometimes life wasn't fair.

"Go back to bed." I kept my voice low and pointed down the hall when Sherlock tromped back inside.

He looked down the hall, then at Eli.

I put a finger to my lips and whispered, "Don't bother him. He's sleeping."

"Not anymore, he's not." Eli opened one eye.

I walked over to the couch and leaned over him. "I'm sorry."

He traced the pattern on my flannel nightgown and grinned.

"What?"

"I'll tell you another time. Not right now." He blew me a kiss. "Go back to bed before Sherlock thinks it's morning."

"Okay, but I was thinking that when you work nights, you should just sleep here during the day while I work. At least until I find another apartment."

Grinning, he tugged at the hem of my nightshirt. "Are you asking to share my bed?"

I swatted his chest, not hard because that would only hurt my hand. "I liked you better when you were quiet."

He clasped my hand and held it against his chest. "That can be arranged."

Sherlock ran up to the couch and barked.

"I should probably go back to bed." The only problem with that was it meant pulling my hand away from his chest. And my hand looked so comfortable pressed against his pecs.

Eli nodded.

"Just for the record, I love you when you're quiet *and* when you're being a patootie." I kissed him before retreating to the bedroom.

If we spent any more nights in the same place, I'd need new rules. But then I'd just be tempted to break them. And that wasn't good.

* * *

THE SMELL of bacon woke me, and I was no longer competing with Sherlock for space. I tugged my hair into a ponytail as I walked down the hall. "You made breakfast."

Eli smiled. "I did. How do you like your eggs?"

He still didn't have a shirt on, and I liked waking up to this view.

"Just however." I spotted fresh coffee and filled a mug. "Coffee! Thank goodness. Most mornings you get it from Tessa's."

"I'm usually either racing out the door or getting off my shift. It's easier to stop and pick it up." He stepped away from the stove. "Sleep okay?"

"I did, and I needed it. It'll be a long day." I thought of all the calls I'd have to make regarding the house.

He handed me a plate. "Sunny side up with a side of bacon. If you need help at the store while you deal with the house stuff, I'm there. I can't promise I'll be good at it, but I'll do my best."

I set my food on the table and looped my arms around his neck. "You are volunteering to help women shop for lingerie?"

He laughed. "If you need me, yes. But I reserve the right to hide in the back if Tandy comes waltzing in."

"How will you help customers find the right size?"

He lifted me off my feet and set me on the counter. "I'd probably need to know the rules about exchanges and returns. In general, being aware of the rules is helpful in avoiding problems."

"I'll remember that."

"So do you need me?"

"I do." I needed him; of that, I was completely sure. "And

as for my rules, I've settled on having just one. To trust my gut."

"And what does your gut tell you?"

"That I'm hungry, and breakfast is getting cold." I kissed him before sliding off the counter. "Now we'll see if you cook as good as you kiss."

CHAPTER 26

*A*fter spending most of the morning on the phone, I stepped into the front of the store. "Has it been busy?" I rubbed Eli's back as I eased up beside him.

"Lots of people, but I think most of them had heard about your house and wanted to check on you. A few people bought stuff."

"Thank you for doing this. Issa should be here soon. She hasn't started teaching yet, so she can cover the rest of this week." I rested my head on his chest. "I've been thinking."

"Hmm?" He kissed the top of my head.

"I didn't grow up seeing people work through problems. Thank you for showing me what a healthy relationship looks like."

"We're going to irritate each other. It's inevitable. But I'll still love you." He glanced toward the door as it opened. "I'm going to slip out the back and see you later."

I inched up and kissed his cheek. "Will you pose for me without a shirt?"

"Just say when." He winked as he walked to the back. "Hello, Tandy. I was just headed out."

Tandy laughed. "I think maybe I scared him off."

"Possibly. He's pretty skittish after working the store for me this morning." I glanced back as the door closed at the end of the hall. "And he doesn't want to leave the puppy alone for too long."

She dropped her extra-large purse onto the counter. "Those Gallagher men are a breed of their own. But we don't need to talk about that. Tell me about you. How are you? I heard the awful news."

Her statement had me itching to ask, but my gut said to wait. Maybe Eli knew why she'd made such a pronouncement. I couldn't disagree with her though.

"I'm okay. It's a shock, and I know the next few weeks will be tough because I'll keep thinking about it. But I have Eli, and he's better than any house."

She tapped a manicured nail on the counter. "Home isn't about walls."

"That's true."

Dragging her bag off the counter, she turned toward the door. "I'll be around if you need me. Just wanted to check on you."

"Have a great day."

Once she was out the door, I wandered through the store, making sure items were in their proper places.

I had more questions than answers regarding the house, and it would be weeks before I had some of the answers.

That gave me time to think, and after yesterday, I had a lot of thinking to do. Since I was building my forever home, I wanted Eli's input because I wanted him to be part of my forever.

* * *

I curled up on Tessa's couch, cradling my cup of tea. "Thank you for being a good friend."

She sat down on the opposite end of the couch. "I was probably too harsh, and I'm sorry about that."

"No. You were absolutely right, and I'm grateful you cared enough to be honest with me. When you left that first night, I wasn't sure if our friendship would survive." I'd never told her why her friendship meant so much, but that would change today.

Shaking her head, she grinned. "It'll take more than a blip of stupidity to chase me off."

"Well, I'm glad. Your friendship means a lot. In fact, I've never told you this, but meeting you was why I chose this location for my store. You are friendly, warm, and authentic. It's a rare combination, and I'm lucky to have you as a friend."

She lifted her mug, intentionally blocking her face. "Thanks."

"I feel like I should explain why those silly rules were so important to me."

"Delaney, you don't have to."

"I want to." I shifted, tucking my feet up next to me. "My mom had issues." I told Tessa about my mom and how my stepmom didn't want me. "I thought those rules kept me from turning out like my mom. I was wrong. I'm not like her. The rules have nothing to do with it." I finished the last of my tea. "And one of the reasons I love you so much is because you make me feel like I belong. Apart from my grandma, and now with Eli, I never really felt that."

Biting her lip, she wiped her cheek. "We can't all have perfect families like Eli did. Some of us just have to muddle through and make the best of it. But you and me, we're both lucky enough to get to be a part of his happy family. They've been awesome to me."

"I'm excited about that too. His mom is so sweet."

"She is. And funny. More than once, I've wished that I'd been her daughter instead of just her niece. But please don't repeat that. My dad would be heartbroken to hear me say that. My mom too." Tessa leaned forward. "I can't tell you how happy I am that you and Eli worked it out. Y'all are my two favorite people, and I'm thrilled to see you happy together."

"Because you know us both so well, you shouldn't ever feel like a third wheel. Ever."

"I'll remember that." She sprang up off the couch. "The brownies are probably ready. Let's indulge."

"Perfect. I'm going to need a lot of chocolate to make it through the insurance process."

* * *

THAT EVENING, Eli and I snuggled on the sofa after dinner. Sherlock was sprawled across our laps.

Eli had been quieter than normal, but I waited until he wanted to talk about it.

"The investigator said it looks like some rags that had been used to stain the cabinets were the likely cause of the fire. The cleanup alone will take a while. They'll need to have the foundation inspected to see if it needs to be torn out. Then the builders would start over from scratch." I hoped they would need to put down a new foundation.

"Rebuilding will be faster if they use the same foundation, but it can be hard to get the smell of smoke out of the concrete. And that was a pretty hot fire." He brushed his thumb back and forth across my fingers.

"I'll let the experts sort it out."

He tilted his head back and sucked in a deep breath. After

huffing it out, he rubbed his jaw. "I have an idea, and before you shut the whole thing down, hear me out, okay?"

"I'm listening."

"Even with insurance, rebuilding is going to be costly." He pinched his lips together. "And paying for an apartment will only pull money away from what you could have spent on the new house."

"I'll figure it out. You don't have to—"

He leaned closer. "You promised to hear me out. I know I don't have to do anything." After pressing a kiss to my cheek, he flashed a smile, probably hoping it would convince me of what he was about to suggest. "The rent on this trailer is cheap. Joji probably spends more feeding me than I give her in rent."

"I'm not going to—" I bit my tongue. "Continue."

"Thank you. So, my suggestion is that you live here, and I'll move back home. Just until the house is done."

"Eli, it could take months. I can't ask you to do that."

He cupped my face. "You didn't ask. I offered, and I'm hoping you'll say yes. I talked to my parents about it today and to Joji. They are all fine with the idea."

"But you have reasons for not living there."

"And now I have reasons for living there. It'll make it so much easier for my mom to do my laundry." His green eyes pleaded with me. "Please."

"Okay."

Eli pointed at Sherlock. "He's going to love the new arrangement."

"You can come over here any time you need a break."

That wonderful grin spread across his face. "I'll be over here a lot, but not because I need a break."

"Because of Boingo?"

Eli rolled his eyes. "Yep. Exactly. I'll come to visit a goat."

I tugged on his shirt, pulling him closer to my lips. "I hope you make a little time for this." Brushing my lips on his always set off the flutters.

Sherlock jumped off as Eli laid me down on the couch. I loved that I could enjoy kissing him without worrying how far he'd take things.

Hovering over me, he teased his lips on my skin. "*This* is my favorite word."

CHAPTER 27

*E*li walked into the store, tapping out his knock as he did. "Hey, beautiful. How was business today?"

I took the time to appreciate this man who called me beautiful as he strolled up to the counter. Not only was he gorgeous; he was mine. There had been no mention of marriage, but forever seemed intertwined with many of our conversations.

"Pretty good. I have a shipment to unpack, but I'll deal with that later. In ten minutes, I'm going to flip that sign, and we can go."

"Since you said you had something important to discuss, I thought maybe we could go out to our favorite oak tree at Granddad's place."

"I'd like that." I'd gotten word back that the house needed a new foundation. This was the perfect opportunity to get Eli's input about possible changes to the floor plan. I had a few ideas.

He picked me up and kissed me, chuckling at my surprise.

"A customer could come in!" What I said didn't match

what I did. Wrapping my arms around his neck, I kissed him again. "You're in a good mood."

"Yep." He set me on my feet. "And I'm curious about what it is you want to discuss. Should I be concerned? Is this a 'we need to talk' sort of thing?"

"I think you'll like the conversation, but I don't want to talk about it here." With my back to the door, I patted his chest. "I do have one 'we need to talk' topic."

"Uh-oh." He lifted his eyebrows.

"Why did you tell Tessa our secret knock?" I'd thought about it so many times but hadn't asked. I wasn't mad about it. The whole knock thing was funny, but it was our knock. I didn't want the whole world knowing about it.

His eyes narrowed. "That was weeks ago. You've been stewing about this for weeks?"

"Stewing isn't the right word, and stop trying to change the subject. I thought it was our secret."

"I was extremely distracted when Tessa asked me about the knock. I didn't exactly tell her what it was, I just responded with 'The E?' And she figured it out." He grinned. "When Tessa and I got in trouble as kids, my mom would put us in time out in separate rooms. I'd be in my room, and Tessa had to sit in the sewing room on the other side of the wall. We'd tap out secret messages to each other."

"Secret messages?"

"Kinda. Mostly we'd just call each other names in knock code. Dork. Nerd. And other words I won't take the time to tap out now."

"You are a dork."

He nodded. "But I'm *your* dork, and that makes me happy."

"Me too." I pulled out of his arms and flipped the sign to closed. "I'm ready."

"Perfect. We'll pick up Sherlock on the way to Granddad's

place." Eli pushed open the door. "Don't forget to set the alarm."

"Right!" I ran back and punched the code into the keypad. "Now I'm ready."

We stepped out onto the sidewalk, and he locked the door before clasping my hand.

While I was a tad nervous about asking Eli to help me decide on the new floorplan for the house—only because it sounded suspiciously close to a proposal—I wasn't going to miss the opportunity to make the house perfect for both of us.

* * *

Eli parked beside his granddad's house.

"We aren't at the barn." I unbuckled my seatbelt and looked around.

He shook his head as he got out of the truck. "Figured we'd take the mule instead of riding horses."

The mule? In my vision of our perfectly romantic evening, a mule didn't seem to fit. "Um… he keeps it here?" I didn't even see a fence.

"He uses it to get around the property." Eli opened the garage and pointed at a beefy-looking golf cart. "The Mule."

"Oh! I was picturing the donkey kind of mule."

He laughed. "Nope. This will get us there quick, and it's easier to take Sherlock along." He reached into the bed of the truck and lifted out a cooler and a blanket.

"You brought a picnic." I'd been so focused on talking to him, I hadn't even thought about eating.

"I did." After setting a cooler and a blanket in the back, he lifted Sherlock onto the seat.

I climbed in and pulled Sherlock into my lap. Talking

about the house under our big oak tree would be even sweeter.

He took a different trail than we did on horseback, and it was a matter of minutes before he parked near the tree. "Let me lay out the blanket. Then I want to tell you something."

I set Sherlock in the grass. "Stay close, buddy."

He ran off after a butterfly.

"Do you mind if I tell you my thing first? Please."

Eli grinned. "Of course. Flip over that corner, will you?"

I smoothed out the other end of the blanket and sat down.

After he'd gotten the other side of the blanket how he wanted it, he stretched out and laid his head in my lap. "What's up?"

"I heard back about the house today. They will be tearing up the existing foundation and starting over."

His brow furrowed. "I'm sorry."

"I'm not. Not at all." I ran my fingers through his thick brown hair. "This means I can make a few modifications to the house plan. Like adding another garage bay and making room for a large work bench and tool chests." Gazing down at him, I waited for a response.

His Adam's apple bobbed up and down as he swallowed.

Had I pushed too far? I hadn't expected silence as an answer. "Or we could leave the garage as it is and put in an outbuilding if that would be better. There is plenty of space for that."

He pulled my hand to his lips. "We?"

"I want your input on the plan. Help me decide on the layout of *our* dream house."

Sherlock bounded up, running right over Eli.

"Whoa, boy." He shifted to a sitting position. "I love the idea of adding another garage bay. And the floorplan you had was great, but I'll give it some thought. For me, my dream home needs one thing."

"What's that?"

Eli shifted to one knee as he reached into his pocket. "Psst, Sherlock."

That puppy sat up on his haunches beside Eli.

"Shasta Delaney Carter, I've rehearsed this question a hundred times because I knew nerves would make it hard to say what my heart wants. Will you make my dreams come true and be my *wife*, my *lover*, and my *forever*?" He flipped open the ring box in his hand.

Sherlock barked, still posing in his often-used begging stance.

"Yes! Oh my gosh, I almost don't know who to hug first." I shifted to my knees and kissed Eli.

As Eli slid the solitaire onto my finger, Sherlock licked my face.

"Sherlock and I are both very happy with your answer." Eli sat down and pulled me into his lap. "I love you, Delaney."

I'd heard those words from him many times, but they sounded sweeter today. "I love you too."

Sherlock pushed his way into my lap and licked both our faces.

This was my family.

When another butterfly flitted by, Sherlock ran off in pursuit.

Nestled in Eli's arms, I leaned my head on his chest. "The day of the fire when you came up behind me, I knew what home felt like. I'd worked so hard to build that house so I could have a home, but…"

His arms tightened around me.

"It's not about the place. It's about who is there with me. Home is about feeling like I belong and feeling cared for, and with you, that's always true."

"That's true for me too. Wherever you are with me, that's my dream home." He kissed my forehead. "I have champagne in the cooler, but I'd have to let you go to get it."

"It can wait. I'm enjoying this, and Sherlock looks like he's in heaven."

"We might have trouble getting him back into the Mule." Eli toyed with my hair. "When would you like to get married?"

With Eli, there was no concern about being engaged for a long time without a wedding date. He wanted to marry me.

"That's a hard question." I laughed at his surprised reaction. "One part of me wants to go find a judge right now. The other part of me wants to plan a wedding and walk up the aisle with butterflies dancing in my stomach."

"Let's have a wedding. I want to stand at the front, holding my breath as you make your way toward me. How long will it take to plan that?"

If I had no other commitments, I could plan it in a matter of weeks, but running a business meant I wouldn't have as much time to plan. "Four months?"

"January sounds like a great time for a wedding."

"Make sure your parents are okay with that, and that you can get leave." I ticked through all the people I needed to talk to about marking off those days.

"My parents will be there no matter what day we choose. What about your parents?" Eli brushed his whiskers along my cheek.

"I'll call my dad tonight. You can meet him over the phone. I'm not even sure how to get in touch with my mom." Mixed emotions about my complicated family prompted tears.

"Do you want her at the wedding?" His voice was soft.

"As crazy as it sounds, I do. But I won't be crushed if she's not there. The day is really about us… and our future." I patted his chest. "Now that I'm not thinking about those stupid rules, I don't feel like I have to prove anything to my mom."

"Speaking of those rules, please… pretty please will you model the merchandise for me after the wedding?"

"Eli darling, I already know what I'll be wearing the first night of our honeymoon. It won't be my flannel nightgown."

He danced his eyebrows. "Let's revisit the idea of finding a judge right now."

Shaking my head, I poked him in the side. "You have to be patient."

Eli and I stayed wrapped in each other's arms as the sun sank toward the horizon.

Then I scanned the small meadow. "Where's Sherlock?"

Eli stood and whistled. Grass rustled as the puppy made his way back to the blanket. "It's getting too dark for you to wander. What about a treat?" Before walking toward the Mule, Eli stopped near the trunk of the tree and reached up to where a large branch met the trunk. Twinkle lights came on. The lower branches were filled with them.

"I'd meant to turn these on before I asked. In case you haven't figured it out, I came over here earlier to set up our spot."

"This is very romantic. I guess that means you didn't ask me just because I brought up changing the plan for the house."

"No, I've had the ring a while. In fact"—he shook his head—"I've just been waiting until the timing felt right."

"What? You can't start to say something and not tell me."

"Look, Delaney, it's not that important. Let's just enjoy tonight."

"Okay." I nodded, but whatever he didn't say was going to keep me awake tonight and distracted when I really wanted to be basking in the romance and starlight.

"While Sherlock enjoys his bone, we'll eat and sip champagne under the lights." He lifted the cooler out of the back. "You're still thinking about it, aren't you?"

"You don't have to tell me."

He laced his fingers with mine. "I had the ring in my pocket when I went into the store that day. I'd just bought it."

My chest tightened, constricting my airflow. "Eli, I'm sorry."

"That's all water under the bridge." He brushed a tear off my cheek. "I didn't even mean to bring it up, but I wanted you to know that there is no impulse in my question. I didn't ask because you called it *our* dream house. I've been planning tonight for a while. When you called and said you had something important to talk about, it made it easier to get you out here without giving away my surprise." He softly and slowly danced his lips on mine. "But when you said you wanted to add another garage bay, then I knew I was in love."

I pulled him in for another kiss. "I didn't grow up with surprises. Not the good kind anyway. You have spoiled me with fun surprises. And I love it."

"I have another surprise, but you'll have to wait." He emptied the cooler and ripped the foil off the top of the bottle.

"I don't know why you decided to talk to me and why you didn't lose interest once you did, but I think it's because we were made for each other." I handed Sherlock a bone while Eli uncorked the champagne.

"Yep. We are. And you're prettier than all those other girls." He winked as the cork popped.

* * *

Eli pulled into his parents' driveway, then clasped my hand. "I hope you like this surprise, and if you don't, please remember that I did it because I love you."

"Now I'm scared. What did you do?" I slid out of the truck.

Sherlock ran toward the door, yipping excitedly.

The door opened a little, and Sherlock bolted inside. Eli shifted behind me and pushed the door open the rest of the way.

A smiling face peeked around the door.

"Dad!" I launched into his arms. "You're here."

"I've missed a lot of things, Delaney, but this wasn't going to be one of them." He held me close a second, then stuck out his hand to Eli. "It's good to see you again, and I can't thank you enough for inviting me."

"See you again?" I looked from my dad to Eli.

"You know when Dad and I went fishing not long ago? That was a cover. We did go fishing, but I drove up to meet your dad and tell him that I wanted to marry his daughter." Eli kissed my head. "I knew you missed him and thought this might be a good time for a quick visit."

My dad wiped his eyes. "There is a roomful of people eager to congratulate you. Come on in."

I hugged Eli as my dad walked around the corner. "Thank you for this. From the bottom of my heart, thank you."

"If you haven't figured it out, I'll go to great lengths to make you happy."

"I am happy. I don't need anything else but you." I kissed his cheek. "We're probably making them antsy."

"Yes. Be prepared to eat. I think my mom cooked enough for an army." He led me into the living room.

Heart-shaped balloons were dotted around the room. The table against the wall was covered in food. The best part of this surprise filled the living room—the smiling faces of my friends and family, his and mine.

His mom hugged me. "I'm so happy he found you."

Tessa nudged her way in. "My turn."

Laughing, I wrapped my arms around her. "You knew. That's why you've been so busy."

"I'm a horrible liar. So, I avoided you." She pulled Eli into the huddle. "I'm so happy for you both."

Joji and Clint grinned as Tessa stepped back.

One by one, our friends and family hugged us and congratulated us. I'd never felt more loved.

Cami walked up with Harper in tow. "I just knew y'all were perfect for each other."

Eli pulled me close. "And you were right."

She glanced around the room. "Who's next?"

Poor Tessa. She was the last single one in the group. Cami would try to play matchmaker, but I wasn't sure who could sweep Tessa off her feet.

One thing was for sure, I didn't want her meeting some stranger and leaving Stadtburg.

"Cami, I think you should revel in this win for a while." Eli tugged me toward the corner. "I'm glad you liked this surprise."

"I love it."

Matthew Gallagher called for everyone's attention. "Does everyone have champagne?" He pointed toward Eli and me, and Patsy handed us each a glass. "Please join me as we lift our glasses to Eli and Delaney. May your love be unending, and I hope all your sons look like me." He flashed that signature grin. "To happily-ever-afters."

We all raised our glasses.

Then I added a toast of my own. "To good guys."

I'd found the best one of all.

EPILOGUE

GARRETT

I sipped my coffee, waiting for Eli to meet me. Based on the conversation at the table behind me, news of his engagement to Delaney had spread quickly.

"I've been in her store before, but I don't really know her. She's not from around here." The woman talked like she was in high school but sounded a bit too old for that.

Turning around to look would give away that I was eavesdropping, so I stayed still.

"Well, whatever she modeled for him sure cured him."

The cute brunette who ran the doughnut shop walked past me. "Or maybe he wasn't the one with the problem."

"You mean *she* has a problem? His fiancée?"

I couldn't tell who asked the question, and it took a lot of willpower not to turn around and look.

"No, that's not what I mean. Just forget it. Have a nice day." The brunette sighed as she passed my table.

"Miss."

She whipped around and smiled. "Yes? What can I help you with?"

She answered to *Miss* without hesitation, and there wasn't

a ring on her finger. Those were helpful pieces of information.

"I just wanted to say how good the doughnut was. Delicious." I stayed too busy playing private investigator to even think about dating right now, but maybe that would change at some point.

"Which kind did you have?" She stuck her hands into the pockets of her apron.

"I had the one with the glaze and pecans on top. So good."

"Thanks." She glanced at the door as a small crowd walked in. "Help yourself to more coffee."

I watched as she chatted with customers and handed doughnuts to the hungry people. Her hair was up in a knot, and I wondered how it would look dancing around her shoulders.

How had it taken me a year to come into the doughnut shop? After being in here today, I wanted to schedule more client meetings at the doughnut shop.

The lady behind me bumped my chair as she stood. "I wonder what Tessa meant. She always did take up for Eli. I'm surprised they didn't get married."

The other woman laughed. "Eli and Tessa are cousins. Didn't you know that?"

"Oh!" The woman flipped her hair over her shoulder as she walked past me. "That makes so much sense."

The ladies were much older than high school age, but by the sound of it, they'd lived here since then. Their gossip had proved helpful. They'd given me a key bit of info. Tessa. I'd have to remember that name.

I went back to watching Tessa.

"Sorry I'm late." Eli dropped into the chair across from me, then looked toward the counter. A slow grin spread across his face. "Admiring the shop owner?"

"Just waiting and enjoying the coffee. I think you're going

to like what I found." I pulled a manilla envelope out of my briefcase.

He leaned forward. "Did you find Delaney's mom?"

"I think so. I'll have confirmation soon. But on that other task, I scored. Big time." I caught sight of that brightly colored apron out of the corner of my eye and smiled up at Tessa.

She set a plate in front of me. "Thought you might want another pecan praline doughnut. And Eli, here's your doughnut and a mug for coffee." Leaning toward the table, she whispered, "I don't want to know what's being discussed here, so if I walk by… be quiet. I do not have the ability to lie. Even for surprises."

Eli chuckled. "Don't you think I know that? I'm not even going to tell you his name."

"Thank you." She fluttered her fingers as she walked back toward the counter.

"Let me fill this mug, and then you can tell me the good news." He walked to the coffee station, giving me another minute to observe Tessa.

She didn't act like she knew who I was. And that was different because the first few months after moving to town, strangers would stop and ask about my dad and my life story. In this area, being related to Beau Henry garnered me attention. Attention I'd rather avoid. He had money, and that made me leery of females who were too attentive.

Tessa was just the right amount of attentive.

"I can introduce you if you'd like." Eli slipped into his chair. "Not right away… for obvious reasons."

I shook my head. "Oh, no. That's okay."

He shrugged. "Probably a good thing. Ever since her broken engagement, she's sworn off men, so getting her to go out with you wouldn't be easy. She's great, though." He pulled the envelope across the table. "How can I surprise Delaney with a reminder of her grandma on our wedding day?"

"The daughter who inherited the house years ago sold it to a guy who rents it out as a vacation rental."

Eli slapped the table. "Yes! That will be perfect. We'd talked about going to a beach somewhere, but we'll spend a night or two in San Antonio. Have you booked it already?"

"I put a hold on it. He's expecting your call. But I wouldn't wait too long to book it."

"Are you kidding? I'll jump on that as soon as we finish up here. Thank you. Back to the first part. You think you found Delaney's mom?"

I glanced down as my phone buzzed, then lifted the phone for Eli to see a photo my associate had sent. "She's in Denver, working at a vegan restaurant. I'll fly out tonight and get a phone number and maybe an address."

"I could hug you."

I put up a hand. "Don't. I'm just doing my job."

"You're helping me make my fiancée happy." He picked up the envelope. "And if Tessa changes her mind about staying single, I'll let you know." Chuckling, he walked out of the shop.

After fishing a few bills out of my pocket, I crossed to the counter and stuffed them into the tip jar.

A bright smile lit up Tessa's face. "Thanks so much."

The idea that Tessa wasn't interested made me more interested. I was stupid that way. But nothing ventured, nothing gained.

"Would you be interested in grabbing dinner later this week? I'm flying out tonight for work, but I should be back by Friday." I reached into my pocket for my phone, hoping I'd at least get her number.

My hope shattered when she shook her head.

"First of all, I don't want to know your name or where

you work or why you are leaving town. If I find out something I shouldn't, I'll have to avoid my best friend until her wedding. I can't go three months without hanging out with her especially because we have a wedding to plan. And second, if I went out with you, I'd know your name." She scrunched up her face, creating a little line between her eyebrows. "You already have a hint of familiarity like I should know who you are, but I'm trying not to think about it. So, thank you, but no."

"Fair enough. I guess I'll see you around." I tapped the counter, more disappointed than I anticipated.

She touched my arm. "I'm sorry. All of what I said is true, but also, I just don't date anymore. I didn't mean to sound rude."

"You didn't. Not at all."

She opened the back of the display case. "Would you like another doughnut?"

"No, thanks. I'd go into a sugar coma. But you'll see me around."

"Okay, well… have a nice day, Mr. X." She'd turned me down, but I did have a mysterious new nickname.

"You too, Tessa." I acted like I didn't see the shocked look on her face as I walked out.

* * *

THANK you for reading *Three Rules I'd Never Break*! I hope you loved Delaney and Eli's story. Find out what happens with Tessa and Garrett in *Two Risks I'd Never Take Again*.

Keep Reading for a BONUS epilogue!

BONUS EPILOGUE

ELI

AFTER THE WEDDING

*K*eeping my eyes on the road was hard to do with Delaney buckled into the passenger seat in her wedding dress. The strapless gown made me want to drop kisses along her collarbone and... other parts. "We're almost there."

She leaned forward in her seat. "My grandma's house was close to here."

"Oh?"

"I'm sure of it. I remember that park. At the light, we'd turn right."

I followed her instructions.

"Then it was the second left. No. The third."

I switched on my blinker and waited for a car to pass before turning left.

She grabbed my arm. "Thank you for driving by here. This is the perfect addition to today."

I turned into the driveway, and she stared at me. "You knew which house."

"I did."

She covered her mouth, and tears glistened in her eyes. "You planned this. It looks so pretty. They've painted it. The blue is nice. It used to be yellow."

"This is where we're staying tonight and tomorrow night. Then we'll fly away to our beach vacation." I leaned across the cab and kissed her. "There is a rhyme that people say for weddings, I think. Something rented; something blue. Something old." I motioned toward the house, then set a gift bag in her lap. "Something new."

"Rented? I think the saying is borrowed." She peeked into the bag. "Should I open this now?"

"Rented. Borrowed. Same difference." I opened my door. "Let's go in, and you can open that later. Wait here. I want to unlock the door first." I punched the code into the little lock box, then pulled out the key and opened the front door. Once I had our bags inside, I opened her door.

She slid out. "How did you arrange this? I'm just stunned."

"They rent it out. It's close to the medical center and not far from the big amusement park. As soon as I found out, I booked it." When we reached the porch, I swept her into my arms. "I plan to do this twice. Tonight and when the new house is finished."

She looped her arms around my neck and dropped kisses along my jaw.

The kisses made it hard to navigate without bumping into walls. But as soon as the front door was closed and bolted, I carried her down the hall.

"Second door on the right. That was my old room."

Thankfully, that room had a large bed.

I flopped onto the mattress, pulling Delaney down on top of me.

She'd somehow managed to keep hold of the gift bag.

"You can open that now or later. It's just a little something I hope you'll wear while we're on our honeymoon."

Her eyes widened, and she yanked tissue out of the top of the bag. When she pulled out the tiny box, she shot me a curious look.

"You can wear it with other things or even by itself. I'd like that too."

She pulled the lid off the box. "A locket."

"There is a picture of Sherlock inside." I lifted it out of the box. "Let me put it on you."

"Wear it by itself, huh?"

"Pretty please. But first, I'd love to see what's under this dress." I kissed her neck, then worked my way along her collarbone.

She stood and gave me her back. "I'll need a little help with these buttons."

"Yes, ma'am." I fumbled with the pearl buttons, determined to get them undone.

After stepping out of her dress, she turned around. She worried her bottom lip a split second before meeting my gaze. "Do you like my corset?"

I nodded, sure that any words I spoke would come out in a squeaky voice. I breathed in deep a few times and smiled. "Yeah. A lot."

I'd never been one for fairy tales, but today, I felt like I was living one.

* * *

ONE YEAR LATER

I double-checked my list, making sure I hadn't missed anything. Dinner was waiting in a warm oven. Her favorite dessert was in the fridge. And candles flickered all over the back porch.

The sun had set, leaving a chill in the air, so I tossed an extra blanket over one of the chairs just in case. I'd already laid out her robe, but it was thin. So far, the weather was cooperating, and I was grateful for the warmer-than-normal night. Mainly because I'd opted not to wear a shirt.

Privacy screens were hung on each side of the porch. I had the perfect playlist ready to go, and the new air mattress was perfectly made and piled with pillows. Once I'd stumbled on her Romantic Nights Pinterest board, I'd chosen one of the ideas and made it happen.

Delaney would be home any minute.

Usually on the mornings I didn't work, I'd stretch out on the bed and watch her get dressed while we chatted. Hands down, the best way to start the day. But this morning, she'd gotten dressed in the closet and wouldn't let me peek.

That had my thoughts in a whirl, and anticipation mounted throughout the day.

The garage door opened, and I hurried over to greet her. Not only was it a special day for us, but I had news to share.

Delaney climbed out of her car, her smile widening as she walked toward me. "Hello, hot stuff."

"Happy anniversary." I pulled her close.

"Where's Sherlock?"

"At my parents' house. Tonight, it's just you and me."

"How romantic." She dotted kisses on my chest.

"Dinner is ready. Wine is chilled. And dessert is in the fridge. Because the weather is nice, I figured we'd eat out on the patio. But if you keep doing that, we'll eat later."

She ran a finger down my chest. "I like that idea."

I led her inside and through the house.

"The back porch has a new addition." She nodded toward the mattress.

"I wanted to be prepared for anything."

Her rules were brought up often. Most commonly when she was modeling lingerie for me. I was almost an expert on identifying the different types of lingerie, a handy skill for someone married to a lingerie store owner.

With music playing, we made use of the mattress and enjoyed each other's company.

* * *

Snuggled under a blanket, I ran my fingers through her hair. "I liked that bodysuit."

She lifted her head off my chest. "I thought you might. And this whole evening on the porch is very romantic. I've wanted to do something like this."

"I figured that out when I found all the pictures on your Romantic Nights board. Romance seemed appropriate for our anniversary, and I have a bit of news."

"Good news?"

"Very good news. I know how hard it is when I work nights because we don't see each other much. Well, I've been promoted to investigator, so no more night shifts. That's not saying I won't be called in the middle of the night from time to time, but it won't be a regular thing."

"Eli, I'm so proud of you."

"It means I won't be pulling over sobbing women, but I'll just have to learn to cope."

"I'm glad you pulled me over that night."

"Me too. I learned a lot about you in those few minutes." I played with her locket. "That night, I decided that I was definitely going to ask you out… even before I saw you in a towel. It just took me a while."

Delaney shifted on top of me. "Totally worth the wait."

At this rate, we'd never eat dinner.

Printed in Great Britain
by Amazon

30680591R00128